At first she kept it lively, jovial, jocular, talking a blue
streak as the gin began its
reserve. But gradually, as
became more and more an
close, cheek to cheek, hugg
perfectly plain she's locke
evening and thrown away
'You *do* dance divinely,' sl
cheek, both arms round my
to mine.
'This is dancing?' I grinned.

Also by Stanley Morgan

TOBIN IN TAHITI

Stanley Morgan

The Rise of Randy Comfort

Futura Publications Limited
A Futura Book

A Futura Book

First published in Great Britain in 1976
by Futura Publications Limited
Reprinted 1977, 1979

ISBN 0 8600 7347 5
Printed in Great Britain by
Hazell Watson & Viney Ltd
Aylesbury, Bucks

Futura Publications Limited
110 Warner Road
Camberwell, London SE5

CHAPTER ONE

I was delivering groceries to one of those fabulous houses in St John's Wood – you know the kind of place, two hundred thousand quids worth of neo-Georgian posh screened from the road by laurel hedges and rhododendron bushes to remove envy and temptation from the passing proletariat. A little world of its own, it was, all neat and clean and tidy, not a daisy in sight on the immaculate front lawn or a weed to defile the herbaceous borders.

I'll take it, I decided, walking up the drive to the front door.

I rang the bell with my nose and turned to inspect the garden. Yes, definitely my cup of tea, though the sundial was a foot off-centre. I'd have that dealt with straight away, can't stand imperfection.

'Goodmorning . . .'

It was not a voice, it was a caress, a warm, exotic invitation to dalliance in unimagineable sexual delight.

I turned, exploded at the sight of her – a vision of blonde, sleep-rumpled loveliness in a frilly white, see-through negligee, not a daisy in sight on her immaculate front lawn nor a weed defiling her herbaceous border.

'Come in,' she breathed, eyeing the groceries and a few dozen other things besides.

I entered.

She closed the door, firmly.

'Nice place you've got here,' I commented.

'But so lonely . . . so terribly lonely. Put the box on the floor.'

'Here?'

'There. Precisely there.'

I stooped, got rid of the box and stood up again and she

was there, very close, her hand on my arm. 'You're terribly good looking, aren't you? Would you do something for me? . . . something . . . very personal?'

'If I can, madam.'

Her limpid eyes undressed me. 'Oh, I'm sure you can. You're so deliciously tall . . . so *strong*.'

'Not bad,' I had to agree.

'What is a beautiful creature like you doing delivering groceries? You ought to be in bed. Come . . . !'

Grabbing my hand, she hauled me across the hall and up the curved staircase, along the landing and into a palatial Arabian Nights bedroom, its bed a vast plateau of sensational black satin.

'Nice place you've got here, too . . .' I began to remark, but she wasn't in the mood for conversational pleasantries. She was tearing at my clothes, ripping them away, desperate for my body, finally coming upon it with a cry of delight.

'Magnificent . . . !'

'Well, I do try to keep in shape. I use one of those Bull-workers, you know, the tube thing you press . . .'

Whhhoosshh!

Her nightie was making puddles at her feet.

Starkers . . . absolutely noddified. Slim as a lad, knockers like melons.

'You fancy me?' she declared triumphantly.

'Like a horse fancies hay, missus.'

'Then let's make it!'

With a whoop she was on the bed, pegged out like a star-fish, begging, aching, desperate for it.

'Erm . . . your husband?' I enquired.

'In China! Come, my stallion . . . pin me to the mattress! Ravish me . . . rape me . . . ex-*cruciate* me!'

'Yours to command, lady,' I chuckled, climbing onto the bed. 'This suit you?'

'Eminently! A wonderous weapon! Drive it deep, my gladiator . . . thrust me to the hilt!'

'Gerrrrr . . . onimo!'

'Miiissstteerr Com . . . foooort!'

I woke, bathed in sweat.

'Miiissstteerrr *Com* . . . foooort!'

It was that screaming hag downstairs, Mrs Maloney, my landlady, screeching up the stair-well. Ohhhh, knickers! What a bloody time to shatter a dream.

'Hellloooo!'

'There's somewun 'ere for you!'

'Just a minute!'

I staggered out of bed, cursing, struggled naked into my dressing gown, went out onto the landing and hung over the rickety bannisters. One of these days the thing would collapse and I'd finish up in her face three floors below.

'Who is it?' I hollered down.

'A bloke!'

'Has he got a name?'

'That's abart all 'e 'as got by the looks of him! That an' flamin' red hair down to 'is knees!'

It was Albert. Christ, was it that time!

'Send him up!'

I leapt back into my room – if you can call a seven-by-seven hole in the roof a room – and dug my watch from under my pillow. Nine o'clock! I was late.

I had my trousers, socks and shoes on by the time he appeared, panting, at the top. 'Hey, aren't you ready yet? . . . Jeezus, these stairs'll be the death of me. I see the old cow is full of her customary jovial bonhomie this morning.'

'Aw, mate, she just ruined the most beautiful dream – best I've had in months. I was just about to roger this fantastic rich bird in St John's Wood . . . spreadeagled all over a black satin bed, she was, *screaming* for it, and I was just about to take the plunge when that faggot woke me up.'

'Shame.'

'Shame? It was a bleedin' crime. Stacked? This one made Mimsie Hardwater a positive fella.'

'Who's Mimsie Hardwater?'

'You know, the Two-ton Tessie that works in the Dole Hole.'

'Oh, *that* Mimsie Hardwater. How come you know her name?'

'Because I asked her.'

'Eh? You're not interested in her are you?'

'Any port in a storm, Albert, is what I say. Things haven't been that plentiful lately that one can afford to overlook a dead cert, even Mimsie Hardwater.'

He was gaping. 'Aw, come *on*, Randy . . . you wouldn't, would you?'

I burst out laughing. 'Not even with yours, son. But it *pays* to keep Mimsie sweet. You never know what she can swing down there if a plum job pops up.'

'True.'

Albert, in case you're wondering, is a student. Of what I haven't the faintest idea, except birds, which, as you might have gathered, is one interest we whole-heartedly share. I met him down at the Social Security office (what we call the Dole Hole) a couple of months ago and we've been going steady ever since. This, being Friday, is pay day, which is why he is currently gracing me with his presence. We lend each other moral support while drawing the tax-payers hard-earned money.

Don't get me wrong – we are not lay-abouts. We are more than willing to do an honest day's work for a day's pay, provided they can find us employment befitting our talents, that is. But as he has requested work along the lines of portrait painter, and I of male lead in a West End theatre production, the Dole Hole has so far not been able to come up with anything even approximating our requirements.

Incidently, Mrs Maloney's reference to his knee-length red hair is a blatant exaggeration. It doesn't reach a millimetre below his elbows. In other respects, though, her remarks are not entirely without foundation. He's worn the same battered old suede jacket and crumpled jeans since I met him, though I do know for a fact he has changed his dun safari shirt at least twice. Either that or he's washed out the spaghetti stains and put it straight back on.

Anything else about him that might interest you? He has freckles, I do know. I saw them one day when we had a high wind. It was one of the few times I've seen his face for hair. Likeable soul. Inoffensive . . . generous to a fault – give you his last Polo mint, would Albert. Not that you'd take it, but he would offer.

And me? – or is it I? Randolph Turpin Comfort – my father was a boxing nut. Nicknamed Randy at birth by parents who must have been endowed with either a mind-boggling naivety or tremendous foresight.

General description: Six feet two, dark, careless hair, green of eye (though not with envy), and heavy enough to take care of myself in most situations, provided there's a convenient exit. Much given to day – as well as night – dreaming about the opposite sex, of whom I am inordinately fond, and I would much relish a ship-board life of unmitigated luxury around the play-ports of the Mediterranean, though with a total working capital of four pounds twenty pence I've got the sneakiest suspicion I won't be embarking upon it this week.

Age: Twenty two.

Birth sign: Scorpio.

Characteristics: Bone idle when disinterested; a tiger when roused.

Jobs since leaving Grammar School: Bank clerk (one month), a welder (one week), council snow-clearer (one day), lavatory attendant (half an hour), ice-cream salesman, assistant piano-tuner, brain surgeon (just to see if you're still awake), meat packer, rent collector, bus conductor and plumber's mate. In short, a misfit.

Surely there's a job for me *somewhere*, my heart cries out!

Yes, lowering and raising the gangplank on my own yacht in the Med.

Ah, well . . . let's get down to the Dole Hole and see what they've got for me this week. And if old Potts, the distributor of largesse and other jokes, comes up with anything like last week's suggestion – kapok stuffer in a mattress factory – I'll above his inkwell up his hooter and spit on his blotter.

Nice place the Kensington Branch of the Department of Social Welfare. Decorated by Cecil Beaton in Buttermilk and Ladies Lavatory Green, it smells like a dog kennel and exudes all the gaeity of a hearse.

All the old familiars were there, queueing for their betting money . . . Bert the Shirt, Hacking Harry, Pick-Nose Pete, Stuttering Stanley and Woebegone Wilf, the most miserable bastard in the Western hemisphere.

' 'Ello, lads,' waved Pete, ramming a free finger up his snoot for a good root. ' 'Ere again, I see.'

Peter is given to these poignant observations from time to time.

'Got anything good today, lads?' enquired Bert the Shirt, so-named because he always lost his weekly drawings on lame nags but still persisted. Well, it wasn't his money, I suppose.

'Yes,' I said. 'Trouser Zipper in the two thirty, it'll fly home.'

'Very comical,' scowled Bert, returning to his racing form.

Hacking Harry obviously thought so. He exploded into a fit of chuckling, wheezing, gasping, spitting coughing, finally coming up with a good one that turned my stomach.

'See your cough's better, Harry,' I observed.

'Chi . . cha . . ho . . chi . . choo . . .' replied Harry, beating himself on the chest, his face now purple in colour and looking about to burst.

'Yuh wanna get something for that,' intoned Woebegone Wilf, happy as a crematorium.

'H.h.he's g.g.got somethin' forrit,' stuttered Stanley, grinning himself stupid. 'H.h.his h.h.h.h.ha.ha.ha.ha . . . hanky!'

The queue moved up a couple as two happy recipients broke away, counting their hard-idled loot, no doubt heading for Ike Cohen's betting shop. I went up on my toes and spotted her – all of her – looking particularly radiant in an off-the-shoulder white nylon blouse that shouldn't have been.

'Mimsie on?' enquired Albert.

'Heat? As always.'

'Go on. Does she really come on strong?'

'As carbolic. Bats her lashes so hard she blows my coat open.'

'You're not tempted, though, hey?'

'Albert, I am infinitely more attracted to the prospect of mumps. If Mimsie were the last female on earth, I could no more screw her than kiss Pete. Not that I ever could with his finger up there, but still . . .'

Now Albert was having a look, at Mimsie, not Pete.

'By God, right pair of tumors, she's got, hasn't she.'

'Ninety six if an inch,' I nodded. 'Each. You'd die not only fighting for breath, but deaf, too.'

'Yeh,' he said unconvincingly.

'Albert . . . by God, you fancy it!'

'Well . . .' he shrugged. 'If you're that sure . . .'

'Wey hey! Hey, want me to put a word in for you? Slip her the nod?'

'Can't do any harm, I suppose, coming from you. Yes, ta.'

'On one condition . . .'

'What's that?'

'That you do *not*, under any circumstances, breathe a word to me of your experience. If I was to dream of it . . .' I shuddered.

Another two sporting types broke from the line and we moved closer. Another two and it was Harry's turn.

'Cheerio, Harry,' I called.

'Che . . . cho . . . cha . . . cha . . . cha!' waved Harry, spitting down his bib, letting go a beaut into the gutter as he hit the door and narrowly missed a cop pushing his bike.

'He'll be dead in a month, the way he's goin',' prophesied Wilf.

'Yeh – and you want to cut out all that laughing, Wilf,' I told him. 'Puts a terrible strain on the heart.'

Away went Bert, nose-down in the racing page, about to divest himself yet again.

'Try Knicker Elastic in the four o'clock, Bert!' I called. 'Very good on the break and really extends for a fast finish!'

'Bollocks,' he said.

'I didn't know that one was running today,' I said to Albert.

'Mm?'

He was mind-locked on Mimsie.

Stanley collected his dibs and moved off.

'So long Stanley!' I called. 'See you next week.'

'Yes, s.s.s.so long, Randy. S.s.s.s.er . . . s.s.s . . .'

'It'll be bleedin' next week before he gets out the door,' muttered Wilf.

'It's cruel to mock the afflicted, Wilf,' I told him. 'I mean, how would you feel if you couldn't laugh for stuttering?'

Now Pete was away, momentarily relinquishing his nose to count his money, though he got in another good one before he reached the door. 'Cheerio, Pete! Keep up the good work, we're rootin' for you!'

'Thno long, Randy! Thee yuh netht week!'

'Your turn, Wilfred.'

As always, he had an argument with Mimsie about his money, just a matter of principle, then he was away.

' 'Bye, Wilf – keep smiling.'

I was next.

'Hello, Gorgeous . . .' she smiled, batting her lashes like a punkah gone berserk.

'Mimsie, angel . . .' I muttered, 'have I got a surprise for *you.*'

'Ooh,' she cooed.

I jerked a thumb over my shoulder. 'See this good-looking fella behind me . . .'

She took a look . . . came quickly back to me. 'That's a fella?'

'He is *mad* for you!' I whispered. 'I mean . . . *stoned* for you.'

'He looks stoned all right.'

'No, I mean it, Mimsie. But he's shy . . . asked me to speak for him. Give him a break, hm?'

'Which part, his neck?'

'No, seriously . . . under all that hair beats a heart of gold, believe me. He'll treat you like a queen!'

'On this money!'

'Listen, his family's got money . . . it may not *seem* like it to look at him . . .'

'I'll go along with that. How did all those rats get to him?'

'Mimsie, honey . . .'

'Now, if *you* were asking . . .'

'Yes, well, you see . . . I'm engaged, Mimsie. I'd love to, but there's just too much at stake to risk a . . .' I smiled secretively, '. . . . an extra-curricular assignation. It's my loss, I know, but . . . darlin', if I could just have the money . . .'

She was shaking her head. 'Not from me, Randolph. Mister Potts would like to have a word in your shell-like. He's got it in there.'

My heart sank. 'Oh, no . . . not another kapok job.'

'He's got something lined up for you. I . . . did suggest I needed a big, strong, handsome male au pair, but he wouldn't wear it. Go on in – he's expecting you.'

'Oh . . .'

I turned to Albert. 'It's a cinch. Says she *adores* red hair. Get stuck in – I've got to see old Potty.'

His chin dropped. 'Not a job?'

'Why not – the day started off lousy, why should it change now? You going to wait for me? This won't take long.'

'How long?'

'How long can it take to say no?'

'OK, I'll wait.'

I mooched off down the room, knocked on Potty's door. He answered it, adding to my misery.

Everything about Potts is thin, even his teeth. He's the only guy I know with *thin* teeth. He is also stone bald, bespectacled, and permanently attired in a navy blue suit so shiny that when the sun shines through his office window the reflection hurts the eyes.

'Ah, Comfort . . . come in, come in.'

His office is a lulu – early grave. Instead of Buttermilk and Ladies' Loo Green, it's panelled in Stinkwood, and I don't think any further description is called for.

'Sit down.'

I sat. The chair is also Stinkwood.

He sat behind his Stinkwood desk, cleared his throat (always a bad sign), and then leaned back and steepled his fingers (the worst sign of all).

'I have a job that I feel will suit your . . . hm . . . qualifications, Mister Comfort.'

I sat forward, expectantly. 'You've got me a lead part in a West End show?'

'Ahem . . . not exactly. As I have explained on countless occasions, that is a job for your theatrical agent – not the Department of Social . . .'

'Oh, he's trying, Mister Potts, but times are hard . . .'

'Indeed they are, young man, *indeed* they are. But while sympathising both with the sad state of the theatre in this country *and* with your own theatrical aspirations, I cannot in all conscience continue to pay out the tax-payers' money *ad infinitum* to people like yourself if – and I repeat – if there is other work you could usefully do *pro tempore.* As I see it, your main objection to other permanent work is that, should the opportunity to attend a casting session occur, your duties would prohibit it, is that not so?'

'Yes, quite right,' I lied.

'Therefore, if employment could be found which not only lay within the scope of your . . . hm . . . qualifications, but also permitted you time off to attend a casting session – should such an occurrence arise – I take it, that in fairness to the tax-payers of this country you would have no objection to accepting?'

'Well, I . . . well, perhaps, but I wouldn't want any more stuffing kapok jobs . . . I mean, kapok stuffing jobs. I sneezed for a week after I was fire . . . after I left there.'

'This is no kapok stuffing job, Mister Comfort. I see from your file that you've had practical experience, albeit peripheral, in a number of trades. You have done a spot of welding . . . a little joinery . . . plumbing . . . in short, you could in all honesty call yourself a "handy man", could you not?'

I shrugged, non-commital to the death. 'Well . . .'

'This is a position as general handyman and assistant to the porter of a large, well-to-do block of flats in Knightsbridge. I have spoken to Mister Berryweed, the porter, and ascertained his requirements and there appears to be nothing connected with this position that you could not adequately handle, a little plumbing in the form of the odd leaky tap or central heating radiator, a little joinery work, sticking doors and windows, that type of thing, a small amount of electrical maintenance . . . you get the idea, I'm sure.'

'Er, yes . . .'

'Furthermore, I have explained your position to Mister Berryweed vis-a-vis the theatre, and he assures me that should you require time off to attend the *occasional* casting session, you may have it . . .'

I brightened.

'. . . with an appropriate deduction in wages, naturally.'

I dulled. 'Yes, naturally.'

'So, Mister Comfort . . . here is the address, it's very local, and I have suggested to Mister Berryweed that, personal commitments permitting, you would want to call round immediately to satisfy yourself that the job is suitable. Is that possible?'

Aw, what the heck. Best to get it over and done with – then get back and sign on again.

'What are the wages, Mister Potts?'

'Thirty five pounds a week, less of course the usual deductions.'

'Of course.' Always of course the usual deductions, to help pay that bunch of idle lay-abouts in the next room! You simply can't win! 'Yes, I'll go round right away.'

'Splendid. I'm sure you'll like Mister Berryweed, he sounds a nice, kindly old ma . . . er, elderly sort of gentleman. Well, let me know how you get on. Oh, yes, we have your entitlement here for last week . . . let's hope this will be the last, hm, Mister Comfort? I'm sure you're disconcerted, to say the least, being so long out of work.'

'That's the word, Mister Potts,' I said, signing for the money. 'Disconcerted.'

Which is what you'll be in about half an hour, cock, when I report back.

I bade him good morning and left, finding Albert slumped in a corner chair, completely hidden by hair, pretending he was a burst sofa.

'Any luck, mate?' I said, kicking him on the ankle.

He raised his eyes, doleful as a sick spaniel. 'Yes.'

'Yes! Then why all the miseries?'

'After she'd accepted the date, she got off her stool and walked across the office. Mate, you didn't tell me she'd got ninety six inch thighs as well as boobs!'

'Honest to God, I've never seen her on the hoof, Albert. Well, that makes two of us lumbered.'

'You've got a job!'

'Not for long. Come on, I'll have a quick coffee with you and then I've got to push off to . . .' I took the slip of paper out of my pocket. 'To Sylvan Glade Mansions, Knightsbridge . . . there to commune with a certain Mister Jack Berryweed, porter of said establishment.'

'What on earth for?'

'General dogsbody job – changing light bulbs, shaving doors, walking poodles and, knowing my luck, unblocking eighteen stopped-up loos the first day, but well-to-do loos, my dear Albert, that's the difference. Makes it all so worthwhile.'

'Posh place, hm?'

'According to Potts. But then his idea of living big is probably having jam on his rice pudding. But don't worry, I'll be back within the hour and give him a hernia for laughs. I just *know* I'm going to detest Sylvan Glade Mansions and Mister Jack Berryweed on sight!'

Just shows you how much I know.

I was dead wrong on both counts.

CHAPTER TWO

Sylvan Glade Mansions was magnificent, a long, three-storeyed building forming three sides of a square, fronted by five acres of manicured lawns, flower beds, tall slender trees . . . and Dan Brogan.

The wrought iron gates were open so I walked through and got practically nowhere.

'Hey, handsome . . . where d'you think you're going?'

The challenge emanated from a green wooden hut just inside the gates. Standing in the doorway was a uniformed cop. He was about my height but five thousand pounds heavier and a whole lot meaner. He had one of those faces that must have done battle with the steel ball of a building demolisher at some time or other, and probably won.

'I, er . . . I've got an appointment with Mister Berryweed, the porter,' I told him, walking over.

'Oh, yeh. Who are you, then?'

'Randolph Comfort. I'm going to see about the job . . . maintenance man.'

'Oh.' His demeanour became distinctly more friendly. 'Aye, I've got you down on the board, here. Can't be too careful, y'know. A big temptation for the villians, this place.'

'Yes, I suppose so. Looks very ritzy.'

'It's ritzy. Hey, have you got a snout on you, I'm out.'

I fished out my fags and gave him one, had one myself.

'Ta. So, you're to be the new maintenance chap, hm?' He gave a grin that would have got him a job as a pantomime demon. 'You'll like it here.'

'Oh? What's so special about it?'

He pulled at his nose, still grinning, and I could tell something good was coming up.

'Perhaps I ought to let you find out for yourself,' he

chaffed, now very chummy, now that I was practically a member of the staff.

'Nah, come on,' I grinned.

'Well . . .' he nodded toward the mansions. 'Fifty four apartments in there chum, very splendid affairs. How much d'you reckon the rents are?'

I shrugged, tried to make a calculation from the three quid a week I paid old Faggot Maloney for my dump. 'Fifty quid a week?'

'Keep goin'.'

'Crikey. A hundred?'

'And fifty, me old son. Six hundred a month, that little lot. Takes your breath away, don't it?'

It had.

'Six hundred a *month*!'

'That sorts the men from the boys, I can tell you. No slag in here, mate. Every one a blue chip original . . .' he gave a filthy chuckle, '. . . and the biggest bunch of nutters you'll meet in a lifetime. Barmy, every bleedin' one of them.'

'Yeh? Not really . . . I mean, not . . .' I fingered my temple.

'Oh, no, not *legal* nutters, sort of eccentric, know what I mean? It's the money that does it, of course. Laws unto themselves, them, but *very* nice with it.'

'Really?'

'Oh, yes . . . very nice. Very generous, too – especially around Christmas. Bought meself a coloured telly with the tips I got last Christmas, straight up. I reckon you ought to do very well here.'

My heart was thumping. 'You think so?'

'What, a good-looking young spark like you, I should cocoa. You'll have them old dames wettin' their panties when they clap eyes on you.'

'Oh, old are they?'

'Not all of them, not by a long shot. Some *very* nice young stuff in there, too . . . two or three models, an actress, an opera singer, a painter, two writers – all very bedworthy.'

My heart was thumping even harder. 'Er . . . married, are they?'

He gave a dirty laugh. 'Don't seem to make that much difference with this lot, does it? They do as they damn-well please. Anyway, the husbands are away half the time . . . business deals abroad, that sort of thing. There's one bird in there – smashing red-head, drives a Merc sports – she's got loot of her own, shouldn't wonder, she's married to a navy captain. Hardly ever sees him. He's always shoving orf to Australia and places. I reckon she's havin' it away with at least three blokes on the side. Leastwise, they drive in here in Jags and Bentleys and ask me to phone through. No one gets past me without an appointment, see. They roll up here and I give the apartment a little ting-a-ling and get the all clear. That's what they pay me for.'

'Yes, of course . . .' I said, my mind a-swim with other matters, like lonely rich red-heads in Merc sports cars having it off on the side. 'Well, I'd better get on and see Mister Berryweed.'

'You'll like him, nice old codger. Deaf as a bleedin' post, but a lovely human being, as the Yanks say. Got some of them here, too. Great tippers, the Yanks. Only got to snap a salute and its worth a dollar.'

'Really . . . erm, what's your name?'

'Brogan – Dan Brogan. Call me Dan.'

'Yes, thanks. I'm Randy.'

'You an' me both, cock,' he chuckled. 'Well, I reckon you've come to the right place, then. If you don't get shafted before the end of next week, I'll eat my tin whistle.'

Blimey. Was I really here or still dreaming? Could this be true!

'You'll find Jack Berryweed in his little office, off the main hall. Go through that middle door and his room's on the left, down a corridor.'

'Well, thanks, Dan, you've been a big help.'

'Think nuthin' of it. There aren't many of us here – just a

couple of cleanin' women who do the halls and corridors, Jack and myself. I'm sure you're going to fit in nicely.'

'Yeah, I think I am,' I grinned. 'I'll let you know how I get on.'

'Oh, you got a special way, have you? I just cock me leg over.'

I left him chortling at his own joke and began the long walk up the drive. Well, here *was* a turn-up. To say I was excited by what he'd told me was grossly understating the case. This was a situation tailor-made for a bloke with my aspirations, there'd have to be a catch somewhere. I bet he was lying through his teeth. There'd be no good-looking birds here, they'd all be old scrags, stiff-necked through walking around with their noses in the air. I mean, you just don't fall into this kind of luck, do you?

Oh, don't you, said a cream Rolls Royce as it swirled round the end of the building and headed towards me, coming fast, driven by a dark-haired bird, who, even in sun-glasses, couldn't possibly have been more than middle thirties.

I stood to one side and followed her past, knowing damn-well she was having a good sneaky look from behind the glasses. What a corker. What class. I made up a note to ask Dan Brogan who she was on my way out.

Come to think of it, it would pay big dividends to cultivate Brogan. I'd have the run-down on every 'possible' in the building within a day or two . . . and then. . . .

I watched Brogan snap a salute at the Rolls then I continued towards the centre door. Stap me, what a set-up. Old Potts would have a heart attack if he knew he'd sent me for a job that I fancied as much as this.

Still . . . better reserve judgment until I'd chatted with Jack Berryweed. There had to be a catch *somewhere*.

I pushed in through glass doors and entered a hall – dark-green marble floor, light-wood walls, gilt half-tables dressed with big bowls of flowers and smelling lovely. Whether it was the flowers or a perfumed spray, I don't know, but it made me go funny in the head. I reckon the top fashion houses in Paris smell like this, unadulterated luxury.

There were three elevators on either side of the hall and two staircases at the far ends, emergency only more than likely. These people don't climb when they can ride. Nor do I, for that matter.

There was an oak door immediately on my left that said 'Porter' in gold lettering, so I went through it into a corridor and found Berryweed's office on the right, facing a window that looked out onto the gardens.

Berryweed was in there. At least I presumed it was him though all I could see was his arse, bent down as he was, putting something in the bottom of a cupboard on the far wall.

His office was neat and tidy, a place for everything and everything in its place. There was a little desk on the right, a filing cabinet beyond, a low cupboard on the left with tea-making equipment on its top. On the walls were boards filled with all sorts of things – keys galore, notices, notes, a calendar – and a big plan of the three wings with each apartment marked with its number and tenant's name. Very useful, that.

I gave a cough.

Nothing happened.

I knocked on the door.

Still nothing.

Then, remembering Brogan saying Berryweed was deaf, I raised my voice. 'Good morning, Mister Berryweed!'

He gave such a start he almost fell headlong into the cupboard.

'Oh . . . !'

He stood up, a bit arthriticky, and turned, his navy-blue peaked cap and steel-rimmed specs drunkenly awry. 'Oh . . . you got here quick. Dan Brogan just this minute phoned you wus coming. Er . . . it is Mister Comfort, isn't it?'

'Yes,' I grinned. 'Randolph Comfort. They call me Randy for short.'

But not for long, I thought, wondered, hoped, prayed.

He held out a rheumy hand. 'How d'you do. I'm Jack Berryweed. Everybody around here calls *me* Mister Berryweed.'

And that's put me in *my* place! This old geezer wasn't so soft as he looked. Tough old boy, but then he'd have to be to look after a place like this. Big responsibility.

Yet despite this opening firmness, I couldn't help liking him. He was the living image of Lampwick on TV – grey, nicotine-stained walrus moustache and all.

'Well, now, let's have a look at you . . .' he said authoritatively, adjusting his specs and looking me up and down. 'Yers, well, you're a nice enough lookin' fella . . . reckon you'd suit the Mansions, but do you *work*? We've had some right layabouts on this job and it just won't do. There's fifty four very posh apartments in these buildings what the tenants pay a lot of money for, and when they want something fixed, they mean *now*, not next Thursday afternoon, d'you get my meanin'?'

'Yes, of course.'

'Hm,' he grunted. 'So the last bloke said, but he spent half 'is time fast asleep in one of the empty garages out back, lazy 'aputh. Well, what can you do? Can you manage a bit of simple plumbing . . . carpentry . . . electricals and that?'

'Yes, I can.'

'I'm not asking for a master's certificate – we get the professionals in for the big stuff – just average runnin' repairs.'

'Yes, I can do them.'

'And are you punctual? I want you 'ere at nine sharp in the mornin's and you don't leave till *my* watch says five, not yours, mine. I won't 'ave you slopin' orf when me back's turned, none of that riddle-me-ree.'

'No, of course not.'

'Eh?'

'I said no, of course not.'

'Hm . . . well, I'm willin' to give you a try for a week, see how you get on. It's my reputation that's at stake, y'know –

I'm responsible for what you do around here. Any trouble and it's my neck that gets the chop, an' at my age that's me finished. So you'll 'ave to behave yourself and do a proper job of work, understand?'

'Perfectly. I'll try and be a credit to you, Mister Berry-weed, scouts' honour.'

'Hm . . .well, when do you want to start – Monday?'

What – and waste a whole day?

I gave a nonchalant shrug. 'How about right now?'

'Eh?' He'd heard all right, he was just surprised. 'Blimey, you are different from the others.' He gave a pleased chuckle. 'Well, why not right now – there's one or two little things need fixin'. I'll give Potts a call an' tell him you're startin' right away. Meanwhile . . .' with a grin he pointed to the electric kettle on top of the cupboard, 'make us a cuppa tea, there's a good lad.'

By the time he came off the phone I'd brewed up. 'Milk and sugar, Mister Berryweed?'

'Four spoons – it's my one passion.'

'Did, er, Mister Potts sound surprised?'

'A bit taken aback, yes. You bin on the dole long?'

'A few weeks. Glad to be working again, I can tell you. Don't hold with this loafing around at the tax-payers expense.'

'Blimey, you *are* different from the others.' He accepted his mug from me, glanced at the tea and beamed. 'Make a good cuppa, too. Sit down there for a minute.'

I took a wooden chair at the end of his desk and he sat at his desk, got out his fags and offered me one. When we'd lit up he sipped his tea, smacked his lips and nodded approvingly. 'From now on, you make the tea. It's better than mine. Live locally, do you?'

'Yes, I've got a room in a boarding house. My parents live in South Wimbledon. How long have you been here, Mister Berryweed?'

'Since these wus built, 1957.'

'Lovely place.'

'Smashing, and wait till you see the apartments. They really are a treat.'

'Do you live here on the premises?'

'Yes, got a room at the end of the corridor. Small but very comfy. All I want, any road.'

'Nice job, hm?'

'It's bin wonderful – the 'appiest years of my life. Nicest people you could wish to meet, these rich folk . . . treated me very kindly. I've seen 'em come and I've seen 'em go and, with the odd one or two exceptions, they've been no trouble at all.' He gave a chuckle and shook his head. 'Old Lady Tarbuth, God rest her soul, was one of the exceptions . . . regular fire-eater, she was. The slightest little thing wrong and she'd be on that phone, raisin' Cane, and, by golly, if it wasn't fixed immediately she'd be back again, cussin' like a navvy. She had a vocabulary that'd do a squaddie proud. Though, somehow, with it comin' out in such a posh voice, it didn't sound like cursing and it used to make me larf – after I'd put the phone down, of course.'

'Any titled people live here now?' I asked, glancing up at the board.

'Yes . . . Viscount Ballymore in 26. Batchelor fella . . . something big in the city. Spends half his time abroad. And Lady Glenbullen in 54 . . .' he grinned, '. . . gay divorcee, Her Ladyship. Reckon she hasn't spent a night at home since she moved in, six months ago.'

'Elderly?' I enquired.

'Nah . . . thirty six or so. Nice-looking woman . . . very handsome.'

I sipped my tea, slotting a 5 and a 4 firmly into my computor memory bank.

'Dan Brogan was telling me you've got models, actresses, artists . . . all sorts of people here, Mister Berryweed.'

'Oh, yers . . . very artistic clientele. Mind you, they're the ones with the money these days. We even had a pop-star here but the others got him chucked out after a month. You've never heard or seen such goin's on . . . wild parties – sex orgies, if you ask me – and the noise! I reckon you could've heard it at Hyde Park Corner. Anyway, he didn't last long, thank Gawd.'

'Quiet lot now, then, are they?'

'Well, depends what you mean by quiet. I mean, compared to *him* they're all dead! But that don't mean they don't enjoy themselves. They have their share of parties and things, but they know how to keep 'em down to a respectable, considerate level. All the apartments are pretty-well sound-proofed, you see – I mean, you'd expect it, costin' what they do. So you can make a fair bit of noise without disturbin' your neighbours. It was just Sonny Jim with his woofers and tweeters that went hog-wild. Blimey, he had enough equipment in his place to stock a department store!'

'Dan Brogan thinks they're *all* nuts . . . eccentric. But nice with it, he said.'

'Yers, well, by ordinary folks' standards I suppose they are. The rich have always bin like that . . . they've always done pretty much as they please, make the rules up as they go along. That'll never change. But you don't have to worry your head about it. All that concerns you is doin' a good job for them – and if you do, you won't be sorry, I can promise you. They can be very generous to people they like.'

'Yes, so Brogan was saying.'

He sniffed. 'Let's see what kind of work you do before talkin' about rewards. Come on, I'll show you around.' He stood up and consulted the apartment chart. 'As you can see, the lay-out's very simple . . . three blocks, East, Centre and West, with three floors each and six apartments to each floor. Apartments 1 to 18 are in the West Block, 19 to 36 are here in the Centre Block, and 37 to 54 in the East Block. So provided you know your 18 times table, yuh can't get lorst. Now I'll show you where your tools are.'

I followed him out of the office, turned right in the corridor and proceeded to a small storage room a couple of doors down.

He opened the door and switched on the light.

'There y'are . . . bagful of plumbing tools under there . . . carpentry stuff there . . . paint . . . Anything you need that we haven't got, give me a shout and we'll get it – providin' *I* think you need it. Right, you can grab that plumbing stuff right now and get yourself up to Mrs Widdlespoon in number 7 – that's . . .'

'Second floor – West Block.'

He blinked at me. 'By gum, you're quick, lad. Good at sums at school, were yuh?'

'Not bad. Used to work in a bank, too.'

'Did you now.' Did I detect a touch of new-found respect? 'Hm . . . well, off you go, then. She's got a leaky radiator, says it's drippin' on her carpet. Just a little tightening job, shouldn't wonder.'

I picked up the tool bag and went out into the corridor, Berryweed following. 'Er . . . Potts said somethin' about you being an actor – that you'd maybe want the odd hour or two orf for whatchamacallits . . .'

'Casting sessions, yes, well . . . if and when they crop up. It won't happen often, I shouldn't think.'

And if this job pays off like I think it might, it won't be happening at all, I thought. Still, it was just as well to keep him primed to the possibility – in case I felt like an afternoon off or a bit of a lie-in one morning.

'You'll be able to give me a bit of notice, though, will you?' he asked. 'I mean, you won't just down-tools and push orf.'

'Oh, no, nothing like that. We always get a day's notice ourselves.'

'Yes . . . well, I suppose that'd be all right. Done much, have you – actin'?'

I do it all the time, mate. 'Yes, quite a bit, Mister Berryweed. Made a film in Honolulu last year. Smashing part. Had to rescue a drowning woman by surfboard.'

'Get away. Bit of a come-down for you, then, this job, isn't it?'

I smiled bravely. 'It's all good experience for an actor, Mister Berryweed. You never know when I'll have to play the part of a plumber.'

'No, that's true. Well, off you go. Come back when you're finished. I'll ring Mrs Widdlespoon and let her know you're coming up.'

'Right.'

Strolling round the front of the building in the bright sunshine, I felt terrific. What a doddle! Easy work in luxurious surroundings, reasonable pay, a nice boss, and . . . and what else, I wondered. What other little perks would the job offer as time went by? The thought brought Mrs Widdlespoon to mind. My first call. What would she be like? Fifty, fat and friendly, I reckoned.

She was all three – plus *very* pissed.

The door opened.

Shock number one – she was in curlers and dressing gown.

Shock number two – she was stoned to the ear-lobes.

'Hi!' she smiled, waving a shaker of martini at me. 'So you're our new handyman. Come on in . . .'

Shock number three – the apartment.

In my social strata you get preconceived ideas about certain things that are very hard to shake. To me an apartment is just a fancy way of saying a flat, and a flat is a flat is a flat – a couple of smallish bedrooms, a cluttered living room, a kitchen so small your elbows hit the walls when you're washing the dishes, and a bathroom to match.

This was *not* one of those places.

This was an eight-roomed palace with a forty-foot lounge filled with eight million quidsworth of antiques and Oriental carpets, and if Mrs Widdlespoon wasn't an American billionairess, I'm Albert's sister-in-law.

She closed the door and took the lead, weaving beautifully, into the lounge. 'Come on through, it's the one under the window at the far end. You've just started, huh . . .?'

'Yes, just this minute, Mrs Widdlespoon. You're my very first customer.'

'How *lovely*! I feel very honoured. What's your name. Mister Bellyweather did tell me, but I'm afraid I've forgotten.'

All this was over her shoulder while she was leading me across the lounge to the radiator.

'It's Comfort, Mrs Widdlespoon. Randy Comfort.'

'Randy . . . Comfort,' she repeated, trying it for size. 'How *adorable*.' Now she'd reached the rad and turned, smiling nicely, the strong light from the windows doing her no favours at all. She had bags under her eyes like black puddings and her face was a relief model of the South Downs. She'd put away a bottle or two in her time had this one. 'What a handsome boy you are, Randy . . .'

I grinned shyly. It gets 'em every time. 'Thank you, Mrs Widdlespoon . . . this is the rad, hm?'

'You know, you remind me so much of my own dear son . . . though he's a little older than you. How old are you?'

'Twenty two . . . well, twenty three tomorrow, actually,' I lied. I thought I'd try this line, see what happened.

Her mouth popped open. 'It's your birthday tomorrow! Well, how *about* that. Let's see . . . the fourth of June – that makes you a Gemini. Yes, I can *see* you're a Gemini . . .'

'You can? What can you see, Mrs Widdlespoon?'

'Gemini people are practical, good-humoured, romantic . . . you *are* romantic, aren't you?'

Aye aye! 'Well, I . . .'

'And shy, too. I *like* that in a man.'

Suddenly from a boy I'd become a man.

'Not . . . *too* shy, though,' she continued with a little suggestive laugh (testing my reaction?). 'All women like a man to *be* a man, after all . . . as I'm sure you know only too well. Tell me, do you have a girl?'

'Well, yes . . .'

'I'm sure you do . . . probably several. So, it's your birthday tomorrow. Well, I think that calls for a celebration drink, what d'you say?' She shook the shaker at me, smiling enticingly.

'Well, I . . .'

'Sure, you will. You do what you have to do to that leaky thing while I get some glasses . . . and don't worry, I won't mention a word to old Bellywarts or whatever his name is.'

Off she went, breaking into song, heading for the kitchen.

I couldn't believe it was happening.

Well, come what may, I thought, and by the looks of things a lot was going to come. Dan Brogan was right so far – this one was definitely off her chump.

I dropped to my knees and had a squint at the rad. Sure enough one of the joints was weeping. I got out a wrench and clamped it on, gave the bush a quarter-turn and the job was done. Not, of course, that I was going to make it seem *that* easy.

I was still at it when she returned five minutes later.

'How's it going, Randy?'

I looked up, not entirely surprised to find she'd removed the curlers and done a bit of futile cosmetic surgery on the face, though she was still wearing the dressing gown – a beautiful embroidered job in white satin. She came bearing drinks on a silver tray and had a magazine tucked under her arm.

'Bit tricky, Mrs Widdlespoon,' I grunted, heaving on the wrench and pausing to wipe my brow. 'It's rusted up . . . ah! there she goes. Phew, warm work.'

'Now you *deserve* a drinkie. Come and sit down over here . . .'

She moved unsteadily to a long sofa covered in yellow velvet, put the tray on a side-table, then fell backwards into the soft cushioning, smiled across at me and patted the sofa. 'Come . . . you must be quite worn out, poor thing.'

'Afraid I can't stay long, Mrs Widdlespoon. Mr Berryweed will be after me, he's got other jobs for me to do.'

'Oh, he can wait a few minutes. Here . . . the best martini in town.'

She handed me a glass and I perched on the edge of the sofa, as though deferential to both it and her.

She raised her glass. 'Here's to your birthday . . . many happy returns of tomorrow.'

'Thank you very much, Mrs Widdlespoon.'

I took a sip. Jeezus . . . straight gin.

She threw hers into the back of her throat and had her glass refilled from the shaker before she'd swallowed. 'Good, hm?'

'Wonderful.'

'Drink up, you're only twenty three once, you know.'

Like hell, I thought, having just made up my mind to be twenty three at least fifty four times this year.

She reached for the magazine and opened it. 'I was just checking your astrological characteristics (it came out as "astlogicle cacktistics"). 'It says here you are ingenious . . . imaginitive . . . have a good command of words and express yourself clearly . . . well, that's certainly true, isn't it?'

I shrugged, self-effacingly. 'Well, I . . .'

'Also you are restless . . . need variety, new faces, new places . . .'

'Oh, yes, that's certainly true, Mrs Widdlespoon. I love to travel . . . if I could. But unfortunately it takes money, doesn't it?'

'Ah, money . . .' she said, skilfully avoiding an answer. 'Says here you spend it easily . . . like to take off at a moment's notice for a week-end away . . .'

'Now, that's *terrifically* true . . . couldn't be truer. But unfortunately week-ends cost money, too, don't they . . .?'

'*But*, it says, if you can't actually *do* the travelling, you can get just as much excitement by reading books about far-away lands.'

'Well, no . . . now, that bit isn't *absolutely* right, Mrs Widdlespoon . . .'

'Aha, it says your imagination will be particularly active this year and that you'll find a way of bringing fresh ideas into a restrictive way of life. Now, how about that!'

Spot on, me old darling.

'What can that mean?' I puzzled.

'Perhaps you've already done it by taking this new job,' she suggested, polishing off her second. 'Drink up and have another. Don't you like my martini?'

'Ooh, I love it. I mustn't get drunk, though, I'd get the sack.'

'Another won't harm you, dear boy.'

I held out my glass and she slopped another dollop in, then refilled her own. 'How very nice it is having a little mid-morning drink with a handsome, charming young man.'

'It's very nice for me, too, Mrs Widdlespoon. You have a beautiful apartment. Do you . . . live here alone?'

She smiled bravely. 'All alone, yes . . .'

'Excuse me asking, but . . . is there a *Mister* Widdlespoon?'

'Ha!' she laughed, 'there most certainly is, though fortunately three thousand miles away. I divorced him five years ago, honey, and good riddance . . . say, do you like music?'

'Yes, I do . . .'

She pointed a droopy finger across the room at a Louis XVth stereogram. 'Go pick out something nice and gay, I feel like having a party.'

Oh, blimey . . . not that I minded, but time was getting on and old Berryweed would be wondering.

Still, mine was not to reason why, I told myself.

I dug out Herb Alpert and got him blowing up a Mexican storm.

'Ole!' she laughed, struggling to her feet, staggered, and sat down heavily again. 'Whoops!' Up she got again, 'Hey, torro! . . . come over here and dance with me!'

Doing a few fancy steps and a lot of hip-wiggling and hand-clapping, I joined her and for one whole number we pranced about like a couple of two-year-olds.

'Hey, this is *fun*! You ever been to Spain, Randy?'

'I've never been out of England, Mrs Widdlespoon. Never had the money.'

'Oh, you've missed something. How those Spaniards dance . . . and how they make *love*! Hoo *hoo* . . .!'

Aye aye . . .

'Pretty good, are they?'

'Fan . . . *tastico*! I go for two months every summer . . . wouldn't miss it for the world.'

I wondered what 'it' referred to, then decided to ask her.

' "It", Mrs Widdlespoon?'

'Naughty, naughty,' she laughed, shaking her finger at me. 'You know very well what I mean. Just because a woman gets a little older doesn't mean she stops having biological needs, now, does it?'

'No, of course not . . .'

'Ah, you *know* about such things!' By God, she was working on me. 'Well, so do those dark-eyed Spanish boys – in spades! They really are *very* good . . . must be all that sun or something. Hey . . .' she stopped dancing long enough to empty her glass and throw in yet another refill. 'Phew! that's a . . . li'l fast for this time of the day . . . find something slower, hm?'

Beginning to float a bit myself now, I trotted to the record holder and flicked through it. 'Andy Williams . . .?'

'Perfect.'

I put him on.

'Ah, much better,' she said, holding out her arms. 'Come and do it with me, Randy.'

I took the prescribed dancing hold on her, but she wasn't having any of that. One bar into the lyrics and she was hard up against me, massaging my chest with her huge breasts and rubbing my thighs with hers.

'Ah, that's just beautiful . . . this is the way those naughty Spaniards dance.'

'Oh, really?' I croaked.

'Do you think me awful, Randy . . .?'

'Awful? Good heavens, no . . . you . . . only want a bit of fun out of life.'

'That's right, honey, that's all I want . . . just a bit of fun. What the hell is life all about if you can't have a bit of fun. I've been without a regular man for five years . . . an' that's a very, very long time. So – yuh get your fun where and when you can, right?'

'Right, Mrs Widdlespoon.'

'You're a lovely man . . . so understanding. Don't get me wrong, now, I don't ask *every* man that comes in to have a drink and dance with me . . . don't you go thinking that . . .'

'Oh, no, I don't, Mrs Widdlespoon.'

'It's just you. I like the look of you, you're a nice-lookin' man . . . *kind* looking. I liked you as soon as you walked in . . . and you've bin very nice to me. And as it's your birthday tomorrow, I'm going to give you a little present . . .'

My heart double-thudded.

She looked up at me and smiled, coyly. 'Would you like a li'l present?'

'Well, that's very kind of you, Mrs Widdlespoon.'

'And if I give *you* a li'l present, will you give Mae Widdlespoon a li'l present?'

I could hardly breathe. The room was going round. 'Wh..' I coughed. 'What could I possibly give you, Mrs Widdlespoon?'

Her eyes taunted me. 'I'd say plenty. Would you . . . like your li'l present now?'

'Well . . .'

'Sure you would.' She broke away but caught my hand. 'Come through, Randy, it's in here . . .'

In the last minute or so the second straight gin had hit me and in a condition of happy don't-give-a-damn I floated after her, across the lounge, down a corridor and through a door into a darkened, curtained room, and before you could say snap we were on the bed and she was pulling my trousers off . . . no, she was *ripping* them off!

'Oh, Randy . . . Randy . . .' she pleaded breathlessly. 'It's been so long . . . quickly . . . quickly!'

'Yes, Mrs Widdlespoon.'

I threw away the shirt, kicked off my shoes, socks, trousers . . . and as I hit skin, she flung off her gown, grabbed me by the shoulders and hauled me between her ravenous thighs.

In I went, straight to the hilt. She let go a bellow that deafened me, grabbed me round the buttocks and really took off. By God, she really went . . . bounced and bucked, gasped and grunted, then broke into a torrent of staccato Spanish commands, urging me on, higher and harder, harder and faster, faster and faster, punctuating each bellow command with a lusty drive of her hips . . . up . . . up . . . up . . . up . . . then suddenly it was upon her!

'Aaaaaahhhhhh!' she cried, driving her fingers into my arse. 'I'm coming . . . I'm *coming*! Oh, Antonio . . . Antonio!'

Eh?

'Give it to me . . . *give* it to me!'

Pow!

I handed her my li'l present and she accepted it with a howl of delight. 'Wonderful . . . *wonderful*! She lapsed into Spanish again, this time into a flood of whispered endearments as she slowed . . . slowed . . . and finally came to a collapsed halt.

'Oh, Randy . . .' she murmured plaintively.

'Yes, Mrs Widdlespoon?'

'Oh, you *are* a good boy. That was . . .' she heaved a

deeply satisfied sigh, '. . . marvellous . . . just *marvellous.*'

'Glad you enjoyed it, Mrs Widdlespoon.'

'It had been *such* a long time.'

'Yes, it seemed a bit that way.'

'I really will have to go to Spain earlier this year. I usually go First of July through August, but I think I'll go next week. And now, dear boy, you must get back to your work, I wouldn't want you to get into trouble.'

'Yes, I should be getting back.'

'I'll just lie here awhile and enjoy the memory. You really were awfully good.'

'Thank you, Mrs Widdlespoon.'

I got dressed quickly. 'Well, I'll say cheerio, Mrs Widdle-spoon.'

'Come here, Randy . . .'

As I approached her she rolled over on her side, opened a bed-side drawer, took something out and gave it to me. 'That's the little present I promised you. And thoroughly deserved.'

'Oh, Mrs Widdlespoon . . .'

'Take it . . . open it when you get home. And have a very happy birthday tomorrow.'

'Thank you very much.'

It was a little hard case, like a cuff-link case.

'Thank you *very* much, Mrs Widdlespoon.'

'No, I thank you, dear boy. Such a *lovely* visit. I do hope you'll come again some time.'

'Any time you say. You know where I am, just give Mr Berryweed a tinkle, I'll be right up.'

Right up.

I gave her a grin. 'You never know, that radiator might start leaking again and it'd be a terrible shame to spoil your lovely carpet.'

'I'll let you know the *moment* it does,' she laughed. 'Good-bye, Randy.'

'Toodle-oo, Mrs Widdlespoon.'
I opened the case as soon as I got out into the corridor.
It *was* a pair of cuff-links – shaped like Spanish guitars.
And studded with bright, sparkly little diamonds.
I strolled back to Berryweed whistling Granada.

CHAPTER THREE

'Where the 'ell have you been?' he demanded, spearing me over his steel specs.

'Wh . . .why at Mrs Widdlespoon's, Mr Berryweed.'

'What, all this time to fix one leaky radiator?'

'Swear to God. Call her if you don't believe me, she'll tell you. It was all rusted up, couldn't move it. I had to oil it and let it soak through.'

That was no lie.

'Well, all right, all right. I don't mind you takin' the time if it's called for. But you'd better get on up to Number 43. She wants three 40 watt light bulbs and her bathroom spray don't work properly.'

'She?' I said, glancing at the board.

'Miss Veronica Dove,' he said, smiling covertly. 'Actress.'

My eyes popped. 'Not *the* Veronica Dove?'

'The one and only, my lad.'

'Blimey, we are in select company.'

'Up you go and quick about it – I phoned her half an hour ago to say you'd be along shortly. She's waitin' to wash her hair.'

'On my way. Light bulbs in the store room?'

'Everything's in the store room.'

'Right.'

Veronica Dove! Right belter, this one – big, busty blonde sex-symbol who'd shot to prominence in the last six months in three box-office smash hits. I hadn't seen the films myself but she'd been splashed all over the Sundays for weeks. You couldn't open a paper without coming face-to-face with that searing, droop-eyed leer, the full, pouty mouth and her near-naked forty four inch tits.

The critics, naturally, had panned her acting, claiming she

had no more to offer than forty four inch tits, and thereby ensuring capacity houses for evermore.

Well, well, well . . . Randy, my boy, you're in!

Number Forty Three, in case you're having difficulty working it out, was on the second floor of the East Wing.

I collected the light bulbs and hastened there in a hurry.

The door was opened by a *stupendous* looking negress bird in a dinky little maid's outfit, short black uniform with white pinny and trimmed with white lace, and a sort of white lace hat thing stuck on the back of her head.

Dark, almond-shaped eyes regarded me quite unemotionally, and for about an hour and a half we just stared at each other. Then I realised I'd put my tool bag down out of sight when I'd rung the bell, so she didn't know who I was.

'Oh . . .' I laughed, stooping to pick up the bag. 'Randolph Comfort, maintenance man. I've come to . . .'

'You're late.'

She stepped back, gestured me in.

'Er, yes, I . . . got held up on my last job. I'm sorry . . .'

'This way.'

She was off down the hall, presenting a spectacle of everlasting delight in her cute little skirt, everything moving like well-greased clockwork.

I followed, naturally.

She led me into a sumptuous lounge, on whose tiger-skin couch reclined none other than *the* Veronica Dove, almost naked in the briefest pair of yellow shorts and a thin red cotton T-shirt, beneath which reposed, in glaring, bra-less relief, the world-famous forty-four inch udders.

As I entered, she snapped a hand over the mouthpiece of the phone she was using, snapped flaring grey/green eyes at me, and snapped, 'Where the fuck have you been?!'

I stood rooted, gaping.

'That old cunt told me you'd be right up half an hour ago! I'm waiting to wash my fucking hair!' She flung an arm in the direction of, I presume, the bathroom. 'Go . . .! Fix it . . .!'

'Yes, ma'm . . .'

'Tess, show him the way or he'll be farting around there all week.'

The negress nodded and led off across the lounge.

As I turned to follow, *the* Veronica Dove turned her vitriolic attention to the phone. 'Listen, my sweet fag, you get that fucking clause buttoned up before Tuesday or no Dove, do you understand? I'm not peddling my cinematographic ass for any piddling ten percent of anything – those days are *long* gone – it's twenty or nothing! . . . Roger, don't *argue*, just *do* it or I'll find an agent who will! Christ, why do I always have to spell everything out ten times before you get the message . . .!'

The bedroom was decorated Early Kink, an ostentatiously large four-poster, covered in white fur and hovered over by pink mirrors, dominating the room and revealing more about Dove's inclinations than a six-page spread in Screen Confessions.

The bathroom, wall-to-walled in pink marble and ceilinged in more pink mirror, confirmed my suspicions, as did the bath, large enough to contain a rugby team and probably had.

'There it is,' Tess informed me, pointing at the mixer spray. 'It's blocked. Come back in the lounge when you're finished I'll show you where we need the bulbs.'

'Roger,' I saluted, de-flowering her with my boyish grin.

'And hurry it up or you'll be wishing you had.'

She turned and strode out, hard as armour-plating, totally grin-proof. Funny, that. I don't wish to overburden you with conceit but it's not often I can't extract at least a glimmer of a smile from the hired help when I put my mind to it. But this one *despised* me!

Anyway, I got working on the spray, unscrewed the head and found the trouble straight away – the holes were bunged up with hard water fur. I loosened it with a screwdriver, poked out the holes with a piece of thin wire, screwed the head back and gave it a try.

Perfect.

Well, she couldn't have faster service than that!

I went back through the bedroom, the old imagination working overtime at the sight of the bed and the pink mirrors above it, and entered the corridor, my progress silent on the deep-piled carpet.

Two strides before the threshold of the lounge, Tess's soothing supplication slowed me to a halt.

'Now, honey, don't let them get you all tensed up, you'll bring on a headache.'

'Goddam sonsabitches . . . that fat prick Gluckstein's behind this!'

'Forget him . . .'

'So help me God, I'll . . .'

'Angel, *forget* him! Let Roger handle it, that's what he's getting paid for. Come here, let me work on your shoulders...'

In the ensuing silence I inched forward to get a peek at what was going on, then found I didn't have to risk exposure – a big mirror on the rear wall did the trick.

Dove was still on the sofa, but now sittting upright, Tess behind her, massaging her neck and shoulder muscles, Dove's head bent forward, her face hidden by a torrent of white-blonde hair.

'That good, honey . . .?'

'You know it is,' murmured Dove.

'You mustn't let them get to you like this, it's the fag's job.'

'Shit, you can't trust any of them. You want it done, you do it yourself. Baby . . .?'

'Yes, honey?'

'Come down a bit, hm?'

With an understanding grin, the maid slid her hands over Dove's shoulders and worked slowly down until she was kneading those incredible breasts, grabbing great handfuls of them and squeezing them like she was making up a big batch of dough for a pie-making session. Dove threw back her head, then slid down onto her spine until she was lying supine, her head on the arm of the sofa, the maid still behind her, working on the boobs.

'Good?' chuckled Tess.

'Baby . . . you're getting me horny . . .'

Dove's hands went to the hem of her T-shirt and . . . flip . . . it was up to her chin! Christ, they were enormous . . . with roses as big as jam-jar lids and nipples standing up like a couple of hazel nuts.

I watched with pounding heart, dry mouth, and a big, burgeoning hard-on, as the maid got to grips with those, rolling them between her fingers and thumbs while Dove squirmed deeper into the cushions and let her legs drop open.

A couple of groans, two or three murmurs I didn't catch, then the maid ran her right hand down Dove's exposed belly, slid her fingers into the top of the shorts and plunged in to the elbow. With a mutter of impatience, Dove's hand flew to the fastening on her shorts and in a trice they were wide open. Now one leg dropped off the couch as the other shot over the back, wide as Harwich harbour, and Tess really started working on her.

Without relinquishing contact, Tess moved from the end of the sofa to the front and dropped to her knees, went for the right hazel nut with her mouth while improving her angle of entry down the shorts. But even this wasn't good enough for Dove, who was now getting worked up to a state of great excitement.

A breathless murmur from her and Tess was on her feet, yanking off the shorts and panties and providing me with a sight of spreadeagled, brown-haired pubes that all but had me off there and then. I couldn't believe I was seeing it – *the* Veronica Dove, naked to the bone, a sight a billion male cinema-goers would have given a year's pay to witness. But what a let-down! Who amongst them would have believed their sizzling, slinky, sensuous sex-symbol was dyke to the core, crazy for ladies, queer as snowballs in July?

Yes, I wondered, who *would* believe it?

Veronica Dove knew the answer to that, almost anybody that was told!

The dirty, underhand plot was in my mind before I could stop it. They'd both treated me most unkindly, with utter contempt! Now, of course, I knew why. And I also knew a way of putting matters right.

But back to the action.

Tess was again on her knees, working away at nip and clit as before, driving Dove bananas. She was moaning and groaning and writhing and jerking and thoroughly enjoying her little self, then suddenly . . . all change. With a yelp she grabbed for Tess's head, flung one leg over the maid's shoulder and pulled Tess's face down between her thighs. In went Tess like it was the first bite she'd had all week, loving it, ravenous for it. Oh, for a camera . . .! I made up my mind right then to buy a little spy camera as soon as I could afford it, always keep it in my pocket for such emergencies. Blackmail? No, it wouldn't be necessary. I reckon Veronica Dove would have paid handsomely for some well-produced eight-by-tens just for her scrap-book!

She hit her climax then – let rip a yip that rattled the windows and followed through with a good half-minute of noisy aftermath before finally dropping her legs deadweight from Tess's shoulder and collapsing in a filleted sprawl, half-on, half-off the sofa.

'Oh, baby . . . baby . . .'

'Feeling better?' chuckled Tess.

'God love yuh, yes.' She made to stir. 'Better clear up before that fink comes in . . .'

'No hurry, he's the idle type. He'll be on that for another ten minutes at least, I know the kind. You had enough, honey?'

Dove reached out and caressed the maid's face. 'No, angel,

I want to make *you*. When the fink's gone we'll have a bath and hit the sack, hm?'

'Right on, I could use it.'

Dove came forward, took Tess's face between her hands and kissed her full on the lips.

That was my cue to move.

With thundering heart, I was over the threshold in three strides. 'All done, ladies, you shouldn't have any more . . . trouble . . . with . . .' I came to a bug-eyed halt.

My entrance shattered them.

Tess gave a yelp and fell backwards in desperate, reflex panic. Dove gaped at me, shocked to the marrow, then instantly collected her wits and bawled, 'GET OUTTA HERE!'

I faltered, stammered. 'Y..yes . . . I'm s..sorry, I . . .' all the while staring at her exposed snatch to make sure she knew I'd got the picture, then I about-turned and strode back into the corridor and into the bedroom . . . and waited, killing myself laughing.

'FUCK!' roared Dove.

For about three minutes they conversed in terse undertones, then, as I knew she would, Tess appeared, flushed, flustered and very unsure of herself, trembling noticeably.

So, fink, am I?

I gave her no quarter, merely a knowing leer and a snide, 'Well, well, well . . .'

Her dark eyes ripped me apart. She was livid, mostly with herself for having misread me. 'What . . . you saw . . .'

'Yes, love?' I said pleasantly.

'It wasn't what it seemed. I . . . Miss Dove has a sprained thigh . . . I was putting something on it.'

I gave her a thirty-two-toothed grin. 'I saw what you put on it, angel . . .' my eyes flicked to her mouth. 'But don't mind me, I'm just the fink plumber.'

She gave a horrified gasp and stepped back a pace, praying the floor would open and swallow her. 'You . . . saw?'

I shrugged. 'Couldn't help it, mirror, mirror on the wall.'

'Oh, my God . . .'

In a real tizz, now, she turned and ran, and didn't come back for five minutes. This time she was *very* subdued, hardly able to meet my eyes. 'Miss Dove wants to talk to you.'

'Sure.'

Dove, now attired in a green velvet housecoat, was seated primly on the sofa, knees together, her manner haughty, hurt, vulnerable. 'All right, what do you want?'

'Want?' I frowned.

'Damn it, don't play games with me! You saw, now what do you want to *un*see!'

Power! *I* had *the* Veronica Dove over a bloody barrel! How much could I make it? – a thousand . . . ten thousand . . .?

I slid her a comforting smile. 'I don't want anything, Miss Dove. What you do in the privacy of your own home is no concern of mine. I came in to fix your shower and replace three bulbs. The shower's working a treat. Where do you want the bulbs?'

Her eyes narrowed and her mouth pulled tight. 'I don't believe you. You're not stupid . . . you know exactly . . .' she stopped, interrupted by a change of thought 'Are you queer?'

I laughed and shook my head. 'No, ma'm.'

'What's your name?'

'Randolph Comfort.'

'How long have you been working here?'

'I . . .' Ostentatiously I looked at my watch. 'Almost three hours . . .'

She snorted a disbelieving laugh. 'Christ Almighty . . .' She paused distractedly and came in on another tack. 'You . . . know who I am?'

'Of course, Miss Dove.'

'And how are you going to *use* your sweet titbit of gossip . . . spread it around your local pub? . . . try to sell it to a

Sunday rag? Tess, get me a brandy, f'Chrissake. . . .' She returned to me, her anger barely contained. 'Well?'

'Would it do any good to tell you I won't mention a word of what I saw to a living soul?'

She didn't answer, just stared at me until Tess had placed a brandy balloon in her hand. 'Do you believe him, Tess?' she asked. Tess stayed close at her side, in support.

'It's difficult to say . . .'

'Yes, isn't it.'

What a bloody incredible situation. This was me standing here, Randy Comfort, the guy who'd been out of work a few hours ago . . . who'd been down there in the grot with Bert the Shirt, Woebegone Wilf and the other berks . . . and who now stood chatting to *the* Veronica Dove whom he'd just seen sucked off by her dyke maid and . . .

'Miss Dove . . .' I said pleasantly, 'I like this job. It may only be three hours old but already I know I'm going to be very happy here and I want it to last. What other chance would a chap in my position have of working in such luxurious surroundings . . . of rubbing shoulders with the rich and the famous, people like yourself? I have big ambitions and not much talent. I'll never be able to afford anything like this . . . and the next best thing is to work in it. So from now on I want you to regard me simply as part of the fixtures and fittings – as someone to call on when you want a bit of help – with anything. I want to be a friend, not a sworn enemy just because I wear trousers.'

They were both staring at me as though I had three eyes and a horn in the middle of my forehead. I noted Tess's hand slide down to touch Dove's shoulder, comfortingly, telling her it was going to be all right.

'Can we really trust you?' Dove asked quietly, beginning now to really *look* at me, seeing me as an individual, a person of some meaning, for the first time.

I nodded. 'Yes, you can.'

'And you don't . . . or *won't* . . . want anything from me in return for your silence?'

'Only what I've just asked for, your friendship. I want to be able to come up here without being bawled at and called a fink.'

Tess lowered her eyes and murmured, 'I'm sorry . . .'

Dove nodded and looked suitably ashamed. 'Yes, so am I.' Then for the first time she smiled and lit up the room. 'Jesus, you really come on *strong*, Randolph Comfort. What do people call you?'

I grinned. 'Randy.'

'Yeh, I'll bet,' she nodded, looking me up and down. 'What did you work at before you came here?'

'This and that . . . a bit of most things.'

'Hm,' she said, like she understood. 'Would you like a drink?'

I looked at my watch. It was lunch time. 'Yes, thank you. Do you have a beer?'

Dove patted Tess's hand affectionately. 'Go get our friend a beer, honey. That's the least we can do for him.'

As Tess disappeared to the kitchen, Dove indicated an armchair opposite. 'Sit down for a minute.'

As I sat I looked up, finding her gaze on me, still wary, still not quite sure. 'You're a good-looking man, as doubtless you've been told many times. You should do well for yourself here.'

'Oh?' I frowned.

She gave me an old-fashioned smile. 'Come on, now, this is Dove you're talking to, not your maiden aunt. You already know you should do well here, that's why you're so keen on the job. You reckon there are rich pickings here, in one way or another. And you're right.'

An amused half-smile. 'I am?'

'You know it. And it seems to me you've got off to a *pretty* good start.'

'Oh?'

She nodded slowly. 'You played me very nicely . . . exactly right.'

'I meant what I said,' I insisted.

'I'm beginning to believe you. Fine. OK, I'm grateful. It's nice to know you're on our side. And if you continue to play ball – keeping your mouth shut about what goes on around here – you'll find those rich pickings will start coming your way.'

My pulse rate tripled. 'Oh . . .?'

She looked at me very steadily, her green eyes holding mine hypnotically, now fully relaxed and totally in control. 'I know everyone in the Mansions. I know their quirks, kicks, needs and foibles. We are a close-knit group. We share confidences . . . help one another in many ways. You hold a unique position here. Though socially not one of us, you nevertheless have access to our homes and to our private lives, and, if you prove yourself worthy of our trust, *could* share in many of our private pleasures. There are a lot of women in the Mansions. Some get very lonely at times. They need the occasional moment of companionship, reassurance, perhaps just a laugh or two, but need to find it without social obligation, do you follow?'

'Perfectly.'

'I'm sure you do. You're very bright. You said you had ambitions . . . for what?'

I shrugged and smiled. 'A comfortable life. I'd like a great deal of money but wouldn't know how to start collecting it. I guess I'm just a lazy slob.'

'You're amazingly honest,' she laughed. 'So – OK, you may be a lazy slob, but you've got certain things to offer that people would be willing to buy. You're good-looking, personable, amusing, intelligent . . . and are probably extremely versatile and imaginative in bed . . . hm?'

I grinned. 'I get by.'

'I'm *damn* sure you do,' she murmured, her eyes half-closing in the famous hooded leer that has driven men cuckoo in countless cinemas and was greatly disturbing yet one more sitting only six feet away from her. 'Maybe I'll get around to finding out first-hand one day.'

My blood erupted. Christ, she was hetero as well!

She saw my excitement and laughed. 'That surprised you.'

'Yes, ma'm.'

She raised an enquiring brow. 'Does the prospect appeal?'

'Infinitely.'

'All right,' she said lightly. 'Say nothing, Tess is terribly possessive. Sssh . . . here she comes now . . .' She continued on her previous tack, but I now had the greatest difficulty concentrating on what she was saying, blasted as I was by the prospect of laying this big, sexy, voluptuous, super-star some time in the future.

'But take things easy . . . just let it ride,' she advised me, as Tess came up and handed me a glass of ice-cold beer from a silver tray. 'Just don't be surprised at anything that might happen during your . . . maintenance calls,' she smiled.

'No, I won't. And . . .' I raised my glass, '. . . thank you.'

The telephone rang. Tess answered it, held it out to me. 'It's for you – the porter.'

Oh, Christ . . .

I got out of the chair and took the receiver. 'Yes, Mr Berryweed?'

'What the heck are you doin' up there? I expected you back ages ago!'

'Trouble with the shower-head, Mr Berryweed – had to take it to pieces and chip off half a pound of hard-water fur. Just about finished now. Anyway, it's lunch time, isn't it?'

'You go to lunch when I say you go to lunch, me lad. Now, get on over to number 5 – West Wing. Mister Nicopopolous. His hot water tap on the barf won't shut orf. He's phoned me three times already. Get goin' now.'

'Right.'

I put the phone down.

'Mister Nicopopolous in Number 5 is having trouble with

his hot water tap,' I told Dove. 'I'd better shoot. Oh, hey, I've got three bulbs to put in for you.'

'Just leave them on the table – Tess can do it. Hell, we're not that helpless.'

'All right, thank you.'

I got the bulbs out of my bag, then said to her. 'Thanks for the beer, Miss Dove, and everything.'

She smiled warmly, her eyes transmitting a message of unbelievable goodwill. 'Goodbye, Randy . . . we'll be seeing you again.'

'Yes, ma'm.'

Tess accompanied me to the door.

' 'Bye, Tess. May I call you Tess?'

'Of course. And thank you.'

Then, by gum, she leaned close and kissed me on the cheek.

I grinned. 'Be seeing you.'

Smiling, she closed the door and, so help me, if I hadn't known different, I'd have said there was more in that smile than just relief and gratitude.

What *was* going on around here!

CHAPTER FOUR

I found Mister Nicopopolous standing on his head in the bedroom. The door was opened by a young Chinese fellow in the white jacket and black trousers garb of house-servant, who greeted me cordially with an unexpected 'Ello, cock, come in,' and led me through into the bedroom, en route for the bathroom.

'The plumber, sir,' he explained to his boss, who, attired in baggy blue-silk Oriental trousers, was up-ended Yoga-style against the wall and looked stuck there for ever.

'How d'you do,' said Nicopopolous. 'Do you do this?'

'No, sir. I have trouble standing on my feet, never mind my head.'

'Very good for you, you ought to do it. Everyone ought to do it. I would like to see the entire world standing on its head.'

'I thought it was,' I said and he rumbled a chuckle, quivering great rolls of belly fat, then came down from the wall with a grunt and stood up.

He was enormous – up and down, sideways, and back-to-front, a darkly handsome, heavily featured man, obviously Greek, though he spoke impeccable public school English.

'You're new,' he remarked.

'Yes, sir, started this morning. Randolph Comfort, at your service.'

'That you can be.' He indicated the bathroom. 'We can't stop the hot water flowing.'

'Two ticks and we'll have it right, sir.'

The Chinese cockney opened the bathroom door and disappeared into a great fog-bank of steam. 'Over here.'

'Keep talking, I can't see you.'

I caught up with him at the bath, a great square job done

in peacock-blue mosaic, eight feet square and three deep. Near-boiling water was gushing into it under high pressure from the open mouth of a gilt, demonic face, the two taps being levers shaped like striking cobras, one each side of the face.

The left-hand snake, in down position, was obviously stuck. As a gesture I tried to lift it but it wouldn't budge.

'Tricky, hm?' suggested the Chinese lad. 'Christ, it's hot in here.'

'Can you open a window?'

'Sure. Er . . . go easy on the tap, eh . . . that's real gold-plate.'

'No kidding?'

'Straight up.'

Blimey, how the other half do live.

I got down on my knees and closely inspected the panelling at the tap end of the bath, found the cunningly concealed fixing screws and in three minutes had the panel off. In I went, turned off the stop-cock and ceased the gushing inferno.

Silence hurt the ears.

It took only seconds to dismantle the tap and locate the trouble – a link in the lever mechanism, locked by a coating of the diabolical hard-water fur. I chipped it away, rubbed it down with emery and gave it a squirt of oil, worked the mechanism until it eased in, then did the cold tap while I was under there.

Five minutes later I had the panel back on and was clearing up.

'There you go, mate,' I said, opening and closing both taps. 'Good as new.'

'Good man.'

He dashed off to tell his master who entered, beaming. 'All fixed? Splendid. Excellent work. I wonder, while you're here . . . there's a small job in the kitchen. Could you do it?'

'Certainly, sir.'

'Billy, show Mister Comfort through, and make him a cup

of coffee while he's there. Thank you, Mister Comfort . . . your speed and expertise shall not go unrewarded.'

'My pleasure, sir.'

It was obvious from the yoga and the furnishings that Nicopopolous was a nut about the Orient. The lounge was done out like a rajah's palace – magnificent silk rugs covering the floor and walls, intricately carved tables were dotted here and there, a huge mound of lounging cushions over by one wall, and the faint odour of exotic incense everywhere.

Even the kitchen, though equipped with all the latest gadgets, was Orient-themed, the cupboard facings latticed and the floor mosaic-ed in ceramic, Indian-style.

'*Ve*-ry nice,' I observed, following Billy in. 'What needs fixing?'

He pointed to the window. 'The extractor fan's packed in. Maybe just a fuse.'

'Right. Got any steps?'

He got some out of the broom cupboard and up I went, pulled the plug out of its wall socket and the plug fell off the cable.

'It's rotten,' I said.

'Can you fix it?'

'Two minutes.'

'Would you like some coffee?'

'Love some. I haven't had lunch yet.'

'How about a sandwich?'

'Nice, mate, yes, thanks.'

'Chicken?'

'Fantastic.'

By the time I'd cut away the dead cable and refixed the plug, he'd made a plate of sarnies fit for a king, all artistically laid out on a gilt-edged plate and trimmed with cress, tomato, radishes and cucumber, just like you see in those Cordon Bleu magazines.

'Is this for *me*?' I grinned, climbing down.

'Sure, why not? Why shouldn't the workers of the world

enjoy the finer things of life. You can wash up there in the sink if you want.'

I had a quick sluice under the tap and joined him at the peninsular bar where he'd set out a place for me in exquisite matching gilt-edged crockery more suitable for a ten-course banquet than a quick chicken sandwich, and I could tell from his grin he'd done it as a joke.

'Wey hey,' I laughed, 'now that's what I call service.' I took a stool and he sat opposite, poured coffee for me and himself from a big percolator and passed me cream and sugar in silver servers. 'Billy what, is it?'

'Chang.'

'From?'

'Fulham,' he grinned. 'My old man's got a Chinese restaurant there. I was born there.'

'Never been to China?'

'Blimey, no. Can't stand Chinese food, either – much prefer fish and chips. How're the sarnies?'

'Fantastic. Have one.'

'Well, maybe one . . .'

'How long have you worked here?'

'Two years.'

'Good boss?'

'The very best. He's a prince is Nicopopolous . . . easy going, thoughtful. He came up the hard way himself, so he knows what it's like at the bottom.'

'Really? That surprises me. I took him to be a well-educated man.'

'Self-taught. Made his first hundred quid pimping in Athens at twelve . . . had ten girls working for him by fifteen . . . went legit – into shipping – at twenty and made his first million at twenty five. Then came the big oil boom, and he's been booming ever since.'

'Rich, hm?'

Chang laughed. 'A bit. He calls this place his "little piedà-terre". He's got a flat in Paris, a villa in Nice and a blinking schloss in Switzerland.'

'Blimey. Do you travel around with him?'

'Oh, yeah, practically everywhere. We'll be off to Nice in a week or so for a few months. Real rough life, I can tell you.'

I shook my head. 'You know something – I'm just beginning to realise I've wasted every day of twenty two years so far. You should see the dump I'm living in – cockroaches as big as mice. And you should see the bleedin' mice!'

'Sounds just like home,' he laughed. 'Yeah, I know . . . that's how I figured it. So I thought – fine, if I can't own luxury, at least I can work in it, so here I am.'

'You actually *live* here, Billy?'

'Sure. Got a room at the end of the hall.' He gave a happy shrug. 'What more could I want? I live like a millionaire, eat like a millionaire, but work like me. When he goes abroad I travel first-class . . . I don't spend any of my wages . . . I get one evening and all day Sunday off . . .'

'And what are the drawbacks, there's got to be one or two?'

'Longish hours, I suppose. I'm always on duty. But, Christ, you can't have everything. And I reckon in ten years I'll have saved up enough to go into business for myself, maybe buy an oil-tanker or something. But, listen, you're on a good thing now, aren't you? I mean this job, should've thought a bloke like you could pick up one or two perks in a set-up like this.'

'How d'you mean?' I asked, all innocent. I wanted to hear it from him.

He smiled guardedly. 'Depends on your inclinations, of course, but . . . well, let's put it this way, since I moved into the Mansions I've picked up a nice bob or two doin' little odd jobs for some of these people – when the boss was away, of course.'

'Of course. What . . . sort of jobs, Billy?'

He didn't answer directly, but turned his attention to the percolator, then, while he was pouring another cup, said, 'They're a weird bunch, mate . . . nice, you understand, but definitely weird. Too much money, I reckon . . . don't know what to do with themselves half the time. They get bored very easily, need a few kicks on the side.'

I grinned. 'What sort of kicks?'

'Anything you can put a name to, from soup to nuts. The important thing is, though, that they need to preserve their image of respectability while enjoying them, know what I mean? Their number one rule is "never foul your own doorstep". Do what the hell you like within your own four walls but don't get found out, understand?'

'Yes, sure. But what kind of things do they . . . ?'

He glanced in the direction of the door, then moved closer. 'Right across the hall – in Number Three – there's a bird, about forty, married to a big wheel in the city. He's away six days a week . . . leaves her all alone, never takes her anywhere. Pots of money but she's bored stupid . . . takes up a new hobby every week but nothing works. Six months ago, just after my boss had left for the office, the bell rang. It was her. Not at all bad-looking, this one, red hair, good figure. I'd met her before, see, the boss had had her and her husband over at Christmas for drinks. Well, she said she was having trouble with her sun-ray lamp and asked me if I could fix it. Sure, I said, I'll nip over and take a look at it.

'Well, I'm working away on the lamp, pretending I don't know the crafty minx has unscrewed the plug and disconnected one of the wires . . .'

'No!'

'Straight up – it couldn't have happened any other way. The live wire was bent right back across the inside of the plug, up by the earth terminal.'

'Must have been her. So what happened?'

'Well, this was in the bedroom, the lamp was standing at the side of the bed. I was sitting on the bed, working away, when in she came, asked me how I was getting on, sat down by the side of me and moved in very close to have a butcher's. Blimey, her perfume scuttled me. Two thousand quid an ounce, it must've been . . . slid right up me nose and blew me brains out. "How very practical you are, Billy," she said. "I'm sure you're awfully good at everything. And what *very* nice hands you have. You'd make a wonderful masseur".'

'*He*-llo . . .'

'Oh sure, no points for originality or subtlety, but she wasn't worried about that. She was making damn sure I got the message. So, naturally, I let her know I *had* got it. You know, madam, I said, that's one thing I've always been interested in. I reckon I'll have to buy a book on it. "And I shall be your very first patient," she said. "I suffer with a stiff back from an old skiing fall, that's why I use the lamp. But without massage it doesn't seem to do much good. If the ache was in a place I could reach, I could do it myself, but . . ." And where exactly *is* the ache, I asked her. She turned round and stuck a thumb in the middle of her back. "Right there, Billy . . . put your hand there".'

He gave a grin. 'Naturally I gave it a bit of a rub and that was it. "Oh, that's wonderful," she said, "that's just what I need. But the professionals never massage while you're sitting up – always lying down".'

'And down she got?'

He nodded. 'And down she got. Next thing she was complaining that her dress was too thick to work through, so that came off . . . then her underslip was too slippery, so that came off . . . then her bra was in the way, so *that* came off . . . and that was it, cock. Next thing her panties were hittin' the deck and I was in there fast. By God, she *was* in a state. I reckon she hadn't had it for months – maybe years. She screwed me to a right old stand-still, I can tell you. Then, nice as pie, she thanked me for fixing her lamp, slipped me a tenner, and said ta ta. I've been back half a dozen times since. Always very nice, always a tenner. No complications. And you're the first person I've ever told, so mum's the word.'

'Wow,' I said, as if Mrs Widdlespoon had never happened. 'Fantastic, Billy. Nice little side-line.'

'Beautiful. Everybody wins and nobody loses.'

'You . . .' I cleared my throat. 'You reckon I could get in on something like it, hm?'

'What – looking like you do? I should say. She may even increase the rate for you.'

'Well, thanks for the tip. I'll, erm, see how it goes.' I looked at my watch. 'I'll have to get back, old Berryweed'll be throwing a fit. Thanks very much for the lunch.'

'Thank the boss, it was his chicken.'

He saw me to the door, opened it and nodded with a grin in the direction of Number Three. 'Why not introduce yourself?'

'What, now?'

'Sure, why not?'

'On what excuse?'

'You made a mistake – thought my boss lived there. I'll wait here by the door and open it when you knock, in case she watches you.'

The crafty devil. He was almost as conniving as I am.

'OK,' I grinned. 'I reckon I'll have to put you on ten percent.'

'I'll take it,' he said seriously.

'Ciao.'

I crossed the corridor, rang the bell on Number Three . . . and waited. Blimey, what a set-up. I chuckled to myself, thinking of the endless permutations of possibilities in fifty four apartments. Not, of course, that the entire fifty four would pay dividends, but even a dozen or so offered spectacular variety and breathtaking potential . . .

The door opened.

She was, as Billy had said, not at all bad-looking, and was certainly stacked. She had on a pottery smock, a loose-fitting coverall, that accentuated more than concealed the thrusting plateau of her boobs, the purpose of the garment evident from the wet clay that covered her hands. There was streak of it in her shoulder-length auburn hair and another smudge at the side of her nicely sculptured mouth. This week's distraction, no doubt.

She smiled immediately, anxious to be of help, welcoming this human intrusion into her spiritless occupation. Light brown eyes flitted smoothly and automatically from head to toe but paused to register my plumber's bag.

'Er . . . Mister Nicopopolous's residence?' I said hesitantly.

'Ah, no . . . Number Five, right behind you.'

'Oh, I'm so sorry, I must have misread the house plan.' I grinned foolishly. 'I only started today, don't know my way around yet. I'm very sorry to have troubled you.'

'It's no trouble,' she said eagerly. 'I . . . er, you . . . you're working here, are you?'

'Just started today. I'm the new maintenance man, my name's Randolph Comfort . . . well, people usually call me Randy. Anything you want fixing, just give Mister Berryweed a call, I'll be right over and happy to oblige.'

'Oh, how wonderful . . .' she laughed. 'Well, at the moment I can't think of anything that needs fixing, but I'll certainly bear it in mind. What . . . sort of things do you fix?'

I shrugged. 'Almost anything. All general maintenance . . . plumbing, woodwork, anything electrical, plugs, switches, lights. If anything goes wrong, just call down and I'll have a look at it for you.'

'That's good to know. I'm sure it will be a great comfort to us all to know you're on hand . . . oh!' she laughed. 'No pun on your name intended, Mr Comfort . . .'

'Randy,' I reminded her.

'Yes, of course . . . well, you'll find Mr Nicopopolous in Number Five.'

'Thank you very much. Er . . . may I know your name, ma'm – I'd like to get to know everybody in the Mansions.'

'It's Dexter. Mrs Dexter.'

I glanced at her hands. 'I'm sorry again for disturbing you. I hope I haven't spoiled anything.'

'Not at all – but I suppose I'd better go before it gets hard.'

'Yes,' I smiled. 'That would be awkward, wouldn't it.'

Zonk!

Though unpremeditated and guilelessly rendered, the *double entendre* nevertheless struck home, her recognition and acceptance of it and amusement by it manifesting itself in the smallest up-turning of her mouth and in the steadiness of her parting gaze, held one beat too long.

'Goodbye, Mrs Dexter,' I said innocently, turning away.

'Goodbye, Mister Comfort.'

She closed the door.

I tapped lightly on Number Five and it opened immediately.

Billy Chang raised heavy black brows.

I winked and nodded. 'Lovely.'

'Ten per cent?'

'You're on.'

His face split in a snowey grin, then he thrust a hand into his pocket and produced a fiver. 'From the boss, he was very pleased. I told him how hard you'd worked on the kitchen fan.'

'Good God. Ten per cent?'

'Why not?'

I dipped in my pocket for fifty pence and gave it to him, taking the fiver. 'Been a pleasure meeting you, Billy.'

'Same here, Randy.'

'I'll be seeing you.'

'Take good care now.'

'The very best.'

Whistling "I'm In The Money" I returned to base.

CHAPTER FIVE

Old Berryweed was brewing up for the afternoon break when I got back. I expected a bit of a blast but instead he looked at me comically over his specs and gave me a, 'Huh huh.'

'Had an extra job to do for Mister Nicopopolous, Mister Berryweed, his kitchen fan was on the blink.'

'Yes, I know. Fancy a cuppa, lad?'

'Yes, thanks very much.'

'Sit down a minute, there's no rush.'

Funny, I thought . . . *how* did he know?

He brought the mugs over and sat down at his desk, taking his time saying what he was going to say. It finally came after he'd got a fag going and had taken his first sip of tea.

'Well, now, made quite a nice start for yourself, haven't you?'

I looked at him, dutifully puzzled, though I had a pretty good idea now how he knew.

'You're wonderin' how I know, aren't you?' he chided, smiling over his specs. 'Well, I told you, in my position I can't be too careful, what you do bein' my responsibility. So I made it my business to find out how you were getting on by phoning the people you've serviced and getting a first-hand report.

With Mrs Widdlespoon in mind, it was all I could do to hold back the laughter. 'Oh,' I said.

'And it looks like you've left a trail of very satisfied customers behind you,' he nodded, demonstrating his own satisfaction. 'And pleased I am to hear it. Well, done, you've made a good beginning. Let's hope it continues.'

'Oh, it'll continue, Mister Berryweed. There's no satisfaction for me in badly done work. All I want you to realise is that sometimes these jobs take longer than you'd think –

like Mrs Widdlespoon's for instance – and the extra thing I did for Mister Nicopopolous. So if I'm not back as quickly as you expect, don't think I'm lying down on the job. It'll either be because the work's taken a turn for the worse or because the occupant needs some extra attention . . .'

'Yes, yes, well, that'll be understood from now on, lad. You do what you have to do and I'll not push you, so long as I know you're playin' the game.'

'I'll be playing the game, Mister Berryweed, have no fear of that. I've taken a great liking to this job and I want to keep it. I've really enjoyed myself today.'

He smiled paternally and patted my arm. 'Splendid. Liking your work is most important . . . otherwise it leads to a cock-up all round, and that doesn't do anybody any good.'

How wrong you are, me old love, how very wrong.

'Mister Berryweed . . .'

'Yes, son?'

'I . . . I don't suppose there's any chance of getting a room here, is there – a little place like yours?'

He looked at me askance. 'Blimey, you don't want much, do you?'

'Well, I was thinking of the week-ends. If someone needed maintenance in a hurry over Saturday and Sunday, I wouldn't be here. What happens then?'

'We just call in the professionals, same as on the big stuff. Or the residents have to wait till Monday mornin', depending on how serious it is.'

'But if I had a little room here, I could be available pretty well all the time. I don't do very much with my week-ends now and . . . well, I'd rather work for my rent, frankly.'

He didn't answer this time, just sipped his tea, thinking about it. Obviously the idea had never occurred to him before. 'Well, I dunno . . .'

'*Is* there such a room available?'

Pause for more thought. 'There might be.'

'What – sort of the same as yours.'

He nodded. 'Yes – in the other blocks. But they're used for storage right now. I dunno . . . I'd have to put it to the owners.'

'Oh, would you?'

'I'll think about it. But you'll need some week-ends orf, surely?'

I shrugged. 'OK, let's make it one week-end out of four. I'll work the other three in exchange for the room . . . and a bathroom, of course.'

'Hm . . . no harm in askin', I suppose. They can only say no. Mightn't be a bad idea at that . . . a lot of the residents *are* at home at the weekends. Yers, all right, I'll put it to them, see what they say.'

'Thanks, Mister Berryweed. I'm living in a right dump at the moment, I was going to move anyway. One thing . . .' I grinned, 'I'd never be late for work. And if any resident needed a helping hand at night, I'd be right here on the door-step. I wouldn't mind doing the odd job at night, really I wouldn't.'

He gave a chuckle. 'Looks like an offer the owners can't refuse, doesn't it?'

He had no idea how much I was banking on it.

The afternoon passed quickly, although nothing of great import happened. I fixed a toilet roll holder back on the wall in Number 36 for a pasty-faced bloke named Gideon who sat watching racing on TV the whole time and didn't say more than three words to me. Then I repainted a bedroom door for a Mrs Manley in Number 12 who played bridge in the lounge with three mates while I was there and slipped me a quid when I left. And suddenly it was five o'clock and time to go home.

'See you Monday, then, Mister Berryweed.'

'Yes, nine sharp, don't be late. What are you doing over the week-end?'

'Haven't quite made up my mind,' I grinned. 'I might fly

out to Bermuda for a bit of water-skiing . . . then again it might be Tanzania for a quick safari. Being a creature of impulse I like to decide spontaneously. And what mischief will you be getting up to?'

'Me?' he laughed. 'I'll have a couple of pints of brown and watch the tellie and that'll be my lot. Nobody ever has far to go to find Jack Berryweed. Cheerio, then, and mind how you go. We want you all in one piece for Monday mornin'.'

Dan Brogan was leaning in the doorway of his hut, waiting for me.

'See you took the job, then. How'd it go?'

'Not bad at all. Did a few little jobs here and there.'

'Any luck with the, er . . .' he rubbed thumb and forefinger together, indicating loot.

I decided to play it cool in case *he* wanted ten percent – for letting me through the gate. 'Tips? No. Why, is it normal?'

He shrugged. 'You never know. They can be very generous if they take a liking to you. Maybe you'll have some luck next week.'

'I hope so.'

'See you Monday, then.'

'You're not on duty all the time, are you, Dan?'

'Heck no, I only work days. The night bloke comes on at seven. Doubt if you'll be meeting him, though.'

Don't bank on that, old buddy, I thought.

'No,' I said. 'Well, see you Monday, Dan.'

I was home in fifteen minutes, the transition from heaven to hell coming as something of a shock. It had taken the Mansions to open my eyes to the state of crumbling dilapidation I was living in. The bloody place was falling down.

Being Friday, dear Mrs Maloney was practically waiting in the hall to collect the rent.

'Ah, there you are, Mister Comfort.'

'Yes, here I am, Mrs Maloney.'

Blimey, she stank. Everything stank. Not of any one smell

but a combination of slum dwelling odours, damp and dirt and cabbage water and God knows what else.

'That'll be three pounds, if you please,' she said, whipping a receipt book out of her dirty pinny.

'Er, you'll take a cheque, Mrs Maloney?'

'Of course not, Mister Comfort, silly of you to ask.'

Reluctantly I took the cash from my pocket and handed it over. It was in her pocket before you could say knife.

'You ever going to get this place painted, Mrs Maloney?' I enquired, looking around the festering lobby. 'Or would the weight of the paint bring the walls down, d'you suppose?'

'No need for impertinence, Mister Comfort. I run a clean, respectable boarding house and what I choose to do with the walls is entirely my own business. But as you're asking, this was painted only two years ago, so it isn't due for another three years at least.'

'And will you have it painted the same colour again, dysentry cream? Beats me how they managed to get that seeping damp effect over there in the corner . . . very clever, that.'

'Your receipt, Mister Comfort, and watch your mouth or my husband will be having a little talk with you. And how many times have I told you about smoking in bed? I found a fag-end crushed out on the bed frame this mornin' . . .'

I didn't hear any more because I was on the second landing by then.

I entered the room, already depressed at the prospect of spending a week-end within these walls, closed the door, lay on the bed, lit a cigarette and had a good think about everything.

No doubt about it, life had taken a sharp turn for the better since this morning. Opportunity had knocked and I'd been right there to open the door. Now it was up to me to consolidate my position.

As I saw it, the plan of campaign was simple, all I had to do was give the customers what they wanted. Fifty four flats . . . fifty four distinct personalities, all wanting something different. So far I'd only just scratched the surface, but the enormous possibilities for financial advancement had already shown themselves. Mrs Widdlespoon . . . Mrs Dexter . . . Mrs Manley . . . Nicopopolous . . . they'd all either coughed up or looked extremely promising, and from what both Veronica Dove and Billy Chang had said, the pickings were there in abundance.

Thing was to take it easy, be respectful, earn their trust, and, above all, to keep my mouth shut, never let any one of them know what else – or who else – I was doing. And I reckoned if I played it like that, the rise of Randy Comfort's fortune was a foregone conclusion.

What a little business this could turn out to be!

Randolph Comfort Limited (or Un-limited), resident maintenance man and general provision merchant, purveyor of anything your little heart desires, provided the price is right. Plumber, carpenter, decorator, electrician . . . and Comforter of Lonely Hearts. Having a hard time, love? Softness is a thing called Comfort.

Old comforter Comfort . . . randy Comfort . . . Call for Comfort for comfort.

Yes, a great little business.

Maybe I'd get some cards printed.

I spent the week-end thinking, dreaming, plotting and planning, and the more I thought about the job, the more convinced I became that it had to be tackled in a proper business-like manner. I really *could* become a business within a business.

So the first thing I decided to do was to start a set of books.

Book One comprised a complete floor plan and apartment listing – two pages of the exercise book being devoted to each apartment. Into this would go a diary of events, what job was done on what day and what transpired during the doing of it. In this way I could keep in mind points of special interest which might come in handy on a subsequent visit.

For instance I made notes on Mrs Widdlespoon's page that she was kinky about Spaniards and astrology, that she'd be abroad all July and August and therefore climbing the walls by September, and that I'd told her my birthday was 4th June.

All important points to remember.

Naturally, at this juncture, I could only compile the names I'd so far visited, but I planned, during the coming week, not only to lift all the names from Jack Berryweed's board, but also to subtley find out, from whatever source possible, as much about the residents as I could, jotting down their likes, dislikes, quirks, kicks and kinks and recording them on their respective pages. This way, at a glance, I could arm myself with invaluable information just prior to a call and thereby make the most of the opportunity.

Book Two was an accounts book comprising three sections.

Section One was again a fifty four page listing of all the apartments into which I would enter the individual amounts deriving from that source. Section Two was a monthly total, and Section Three a grand total. This, of course, was purely for my own interest, but it would please me to know, at the end of, say, a year, just what the job was worth.

Fine . . . I got that done.

The next thing was to convert the cuff-links into cash. I wasn't going to end up with a drawerful of presents I'd never wear or use, and since I regarded the cuff-links as only being a delicate way of paying for service, I felt no compunction about flogging them.

I went to six second-hand jewellery places for quotes before accepting an offer. They didn't vary all that much, the lowest being thirty five quid and the highest forty three, but the extra eight pounds made the Saturday afternoon effort very worthwhile and I was tickled pink with the result.

And who wouldn't be?

In one day – my very first day – at the Mansions, I'd earned an incredible forty nine pounds (less 50p to Billy) in tips, plus seven pounds in wages (less Tax etc. of course), bringing the total to about fifty four quid. Tickled pink? I was bright crimson!

I celebrated the occasion with a couple of pints at my local, pie-and-chips at Alf's caff on the High Street, and the latest Swedish import 'Lust And Found' at the Windmill. It was terrible.

Sunday I slept late and went to bed early, building up my strength for Monday.

Good job I did.

I certainly needed it.

CHAPTER SIX

'Morning, Dan.'

' 'Ello, mate . . . good week-end?'

'Very quiet. Flew down to St Trop for a swim, on to Rome for lunch, back to Paris for the Follies, then home early. I was in bed by two.'

'Yeh, if only,' he grinned. 'Mind you, it's what some of this lot do.'

'Hey, I meant to ask you, who was the corker in the cream Rolls and sunglasses? She drove out as I walked in on Friday.'

His face split. 'That, me old son, is Lady Lovey Glenbullen . . . Number Fifty Four.'

'The gay divorcee?'

'Oh, Jack told you, hm? Yes, that's the lady. Nice?'

'Beautiful. Just how gay is she, Dan?'

'Oh, she swings, son, swings.'

'Dan, look . . .' I edged closer, lowered my voice. 'As I'm now working here full time, I reckon it's only right I should know as much about the residents as possible, know what I mean?'

His smirk told me I didn't have to draw pictures.

'Of *course* it's right,' he nodded, mock earnest, 'now you're one of the family. Anythin' you want to know, just ask.'

'I was wondering . . . if you'd like to jot a few notes down on a piece of paper, a sort of brief resumé of each occupant.'

His eyes narrowed, humorously suspicious. 'Now what are you up to, my lad?'

'Oh, nothing . . . it's just that I have a lousy memory and seeing it down on paper would help me fix them all in my mind. I mean, I'm going to be dealing with them inside their apartments and I'd like to know what I'm walking into. If, for instance, one of them's bad-tempered first thing in the morning, I want to know about it so I can avoid trouble.'

'Yeah, well, that makes good sense.'

'Just a word or two, giving their essential characteristics . . . any special, well, quirks . . . would do. I'm sure you know what I'll need. I'd er, cover your time and trouble.'

'Oh, no need for that, mate,' he said, meaning 'a couple of quid will do very nicely'. 'Yes, I'll knock that out for you.'

I thanked him and moved on, reaching Berryweed's office dead on nine.

'Morning, Mister Berryweed.'

Seated at his desk, he looked up, then made a big thing of pulling out his pocket watch and checking the time. 'Spot on,' he beamed. 'You're making a real good start, lad. Got a few jobs for you already . . . don't know what happened over the week-end, everything seemed to go wrong. Never had so many calls over one week-end.'

Aye aye! Had Veronica Dove been at it already?

'What needs doing?' I asked casually, my heart banging a bit.

He consulted his jotter. 'You'd better go up to Forty Eight first, that's Miss Rachel Roget, the French painter lady. She's in a right mess – her bedroom curtains fell down this morning. Her maid went to draw them back and the 'ole lot fell orf the wall. Forty Eight's on the second floor, East Wing. Pop downstairs to Forty when you're finished there, that's Miss Suzie Drew, the model. She won't be there but her maid will. Her name's Frances.'

'I'd better write all this down or I'll forget,' I said.

He passed me pencil and paper.

'What's wrong in Forty?' I asked, scribbling away.

'The bathroom cabinet fell orf the wall. Don't know what's been goin' on around here, we must have poltergeists or somethin'. Everything seems to be fallin' orf the walls. Very funny, I must say.'

Very, I thought, hiding a grin.

'Well, it just shows you I was right about the week-ends, Mister Berryweed. And it could've been more serious than curtains and a cabinet.'

'Yes, I'm lookin' into the business of you livin' in. I'll be contactin' the owners this morning.'

'Great. I don't suppose they'd make up their minds right away, though, would they?'

He gave a shrug. 'I can't say what they'll do. But I'll be recommendin' it as a good idea, though.'

'Thanks, Mister Berryweed. Well, I'll get my tools and be off. Looks like a busy little day.'

I've made some understatements in my life, but that one was ridiculous.

I collected my carpentry stuff and hot-footed it up to 48, rang the bell and waited, quietly whistling 'Everything's Coming Up Roses'. *Had* Veronica Dove been spreading the gospel over the week-end – or was this rash of jobs just coincidence? No doubt the answer would be revealed sometime during the day.

The door opened.

She was a quiet, mousey little thing in black and white maid's outfit, the usual domestic's garb for the building, I was to find out.

'M'sieur?'

I gave her a smile. 'Randolph Comfort, maintenance man. I, er, believe you had something fall down this morning. I've come to pull . . . put them up.'

If she got the crack she wasn't letting on. Stiff-faced, she muttered, 'Ah, oui, ze curtains. Please to come in.'

The apartment smelled of paint, hardly surprising, madam being a painter.

She led me through into a lounge that was more like an art gallery. There must have been thirty, forty paintings on the white walls. Beautiful place, though . . . lovely furniture and a lot of *objets d'art*, as the French say.

Down the usual corridor we went, passing a couple of doors

before finally entering the master bedroom, done out in pink and white, the bed mounted on a low plinth to emphasise its importance.

'Ah, yes, you have got trouble,' I remarked, noting the pink satin drapes lying in a heap under the window and the holes in the wall where the screws had been. 'Would you by any chance have something I could stand on . . . your shoulders, maybe?' I grinned.

No sense of humour this one. 'I will get you a chair.'

While she was gone, I unhooked the curtains from the rail and got things generally sorted out, pondering on how the rail could have fallen off the wall without bringing four tons of plaster with it.

The screws had been well-plugged and the plugs were still in the wall, neat as ninepence. All very strange, unless . . . unless the screws had been purposely withdrawn to the last turn of their thread, so that a good yank would bring the whole lot down!

Was it possible someone would go to all that trouble to get me in here? Nah, don't be daft, I thought. It just couldn't be. Somehow the screws had worked loose by themselves.

I got the rail clear of the curtains, then inspected the screws that were still held in the brackets. Curioser and curioser . . . they were all clean as new, no bits of plugging stuck to them or anything.

The maid returned, bringing a wooden chair.

'Er . . . what exactly happened?' I asked her. 'You just opened the curtains and they fell down?'

'Yes, m'sieur, I pull ze cord and they fall down.'

'OK, thanks, love . . . I'll bring the chair through when I'm finished.'

She departed and I started.

The job itself was easy, just screwing the screws back in, and I'd been working quietly away for a couple of minutes, still puzzled as to how they could have just fallen out of the wall, when I got a sixth-sense tingle at the back of my neck that somebody was watching me.

I turned round . . . and almost fell off the chair.

A slim, dark-haired bird in her early thirties, dressed very casually in a multi-coloured blouse and black, paint-spattered slacks, was leaning against the wall by the door, smoking a cigarette and watching me with a lazy, amused smile, as though she was enjoying some private joke.

She was no raving beauty facially, but there was something about her that stirred me instantly.

She was a *very* sexy-looking woman.

'Good morning,' she said, in a low, slightly-accented, bed-warm voice, her eyes and mouth holding the smile. 'Can you fix it?'

'Yes, no trouble. Er . . . Miss Roget, is it?'

'That's right. And what's your name?'

I had the strongest feeling she already knew.

'Comfort,' I said. 'Randolph Comfort. I'm the new maintenance man . . . I started Friday.'

'Do you need any help?'

'With this? Well, the rail *is* a bit whippy . . .'

'Would you like me to hold it for you?'

Jeezus, *would* I?

'Well . . . thank you very much, yes, it'd be a big help.'

She pushed away from the wall and came over, paused at a side table to smash out her fag in an ashtray, then came up close. I smiled down at her, the old ticker breaking into a rhumba, excited by her easy-going approach and the fact that she was *there*, bothering to help me.

Surely this was the Dove's doing?

'What would you like me to do?' she asked, taking hold of the rail end.

'If you could just hold it up, Miss, take the weight, I can get a couple more screws in and that should do it.'

'Like this,' she said, raising the rail high above her head

and almost bursting her blouse in the process. From where I was standing it was blindingly obvious she had no bra on.

'Lovely,' I croaked and stood up, wondering if my legs would hold me.

While I was screwing away, I knew her eyes were on me, so I took my time and gave her a good eyeful. Being summer, all I was wearing was a thin blue shirt, open almost to the waist, and a pair of dark blue cotton jeans, having decided I'd rather risk dirtying my own clothes than wear a pair of sexless overalls. I saw it as a profitable, long-term investment.

'Women are generally so useless at these jobs,' she remarked, her husky, cutely accented voice bathing me like warm oil. 'They have neither the aptitude nor a man's muscular strength to do them successfully.'

What a load of old cobblers. Women can do anything they put their conniving little minds to.

'No, thank heaven,' I grinned. '*Vive la difference*, as the French say.'

'Oh, you speak French?'

'I'm afraid not, only school boy stuff . . . though I've a mind to learn it. I think it's a very romantic language.'

'Ah, you are a romantic,' she nodded. 'That is good. But where would you use your romantic French when you have learned it?'

I gave a shrug. 'I'd have to find myself a French bird, wouldn't I, otherwise I'd be flogging a dead horse.'

She laughed brightly. 'Yes, I think so.'

I finished another screw, got down, moved the chair along, and climbed up again.

'Tell me . . .' she said, 'do you play a lot of sports? You look very strong. You have excellent muscle definition.'

I looked down at her, matching the smile in her eyes. 'I do?'

'Forgive me for being personal, but . . . as an artist I am naturally interested in the human form.'

'Oh, of course. I don't mind in the least, it's very flattering, thank you. No, I don't play sports now. I played everything at school but not since. How about you?'

I was going to remark on her muscle definition but, remembering my rule to play it cool, didn't. Let the pitch come from them, then there could be no kick-back.

'I ski quite a lot, snow in the winter, water in the summer. I adore it. Have you ever tried it?'

'No, I'm afraid not. That again is something I'd *like* to take up, but . . .' I shrugged. 'Maybe one day I'll get around to doing *all* the things I want to do.'

'And what are they?'

You, for a start, love, I sighed inwardly.

'Oh . . . a million things. I'd like to have my own yacht in the Med, for instance . . .'

She laughed. 'Now, that's what I call ambition. Thinking big is certainly not one of your problems.'

'Thinking is never the problem, it's the doing, isn't it? It doesn't cost anything to day-dream.'

'Perhaps not, but the thinking must always come before the doing, so at least it's a start. Many people are unable or are afraid to even do the thinking.'

'Oh, I'm a past-master at day-dreaming. Pity it wasn't a school subject, I'd have probably graduated with honours.'

'And what do you day-dream about, Randolph?'

If only you knew, Miss Roget.

'People call me Randy,' I smiled.

'Do they, Randy . . . ?'

The way she said it sent a shiver up my spine.

'Oh, all sorts of things . . . pure escapism, of course.'

'From what?'

I shrugged again, then laughed. 'I was going to say from my dreary, work-a-day world, but that no longer applies, not since I took this job. This has been a real saver for me, I love it.'

'How very nice. And what do you like particularly about it?'

I looked down at her. 'The people. I've never worked for such lovely bosses.'

'You mean the owners? I've never met . . .'

'No, I mean the residents, Miss Roget. You're my bosses, you know. You can have me fired in a minute if I don't do a good job.'

She tilted her head, thinking about it. 'Yes, I suppose you're right.'

'And it gives me great pleasure to be working for people like you . . . and Miss Veronica Dove. You know Miss Dove. I presume?'

'Oh, yes, very well. We're great friends.'

'I was up there on Friday . . . I fixed her shower spray.'

'Yes, she told . . . she did mention there was somebody new on the maintenance staff . . .'

Ha ha! Gotcha!

'I'm delighted they finally got someone,' she went on, hurriedly I thought. 'There's been no one here for over a week.'

'What was the last chap like?'

'Miserable,' she laughed. 'Short, fat, bald and grouchy.'

And I wonder who got rid of him!

I put the final screw in and stepped down. 'There . . . that should hold it.'

'How tall are you?'

Eh?

'Six two, miss.'

'And beautifully proportioned.' Her eyes swept over my shoulders, chest . . . down to my feet. 'Randy . . . what do you do in your spare time?'

'I . . .' Oh boy. 'Not much, actually . . . I live alone. I read, go to the pictures . . . not much.'

She crossed to the bed and picked up the curtain. 'How would you like to earn a little pin-money after you finish work one evening?'

My blood exploded.

'I'd be very interested, miss. Erm . . . doing what sort of . . .'

'Modelling.' She turned, handed me the curtain, her eyes on mine, voice softly imploring. 'I need a male model for a painting I'm doing. Are you still interested?'

I gulped. 'Very . . . if you think I'll do.'

'You will do beautifully. I will pay you two pounds an hour with a guaranteed minimum of three hours a sitting, how does that sound?'

'Wonderful,' I laughed. 'Wow . . .'

'Good. Could we make a start, say, tomorrow evening? What time do you finish work?'

'At five.'

'Where do you normally eat dinner?'

'At a caff on the High Street.'

'If we work later than seven you will eat dinner here. I will have something cooked during the day, a casserole, perhaps, you would like that?'

'Fantastic.'

'Good. I will see you tomorrow at five, then. Goodbye till then.'

She made for the door.

'Goodbye, miss . . . oh, Miss Roget . . .'

She turned, smiling happily, 'Yes, Randy . . . ?'

'Do you mind if I ask what the painting's going to be?'

'You will see when you arrive. I want it to be a surprise.'

'Yes, certainly. It was just that . . . well, I was wondering about clothes. Is there anything special you'd like me to wear?'

Stap me, those eyes turned to smouldering coals. 'No,' she murmured huskily, 'nothing special. You'll be just lovely as you are.'

Ten minutes later I was down at Apartment Forty, still floating on Cloud Neuf. Two pounds an hour . . . three hours minimum . . . six quid a trip *and* her for company. What was happening to me?

Son, I thought, any time now you're going to wake up and discover it's all been a beautiful dream . . . and then you're going to seal the door and the window, turn on the gas and finish it all forever.

But how *could* it be a dream? This *was* a real carpet I was standing on . . . in a real hall . . . pressing a real bell button. I was *here* . . . in the Mansions . . . waiting for a real door to open . . .

It opened.

'Oh, hello, have you come to fix the cabinet?'

Another maid, blonde this time, and infinitely happier than the little French mouse. London, from her accent. Not ravishingly beautiful but it was all there. Five foot four, eyes of blue, hair tied back in a roll and very good legs, most of which I could see because her uniform was extremely short.

'Randy Comfort . . . at your service, miss,' I bowed.

She giggled. 'You're joking!'

'No, deadly serious.'

I stepped into the hall, and whispered, 'Anyone at home?'

She closed the door and nodded. 'Yes!'

'Who?'

'Me!'

She giggled again and took off down the hall. I gave her a count of three and followed. *Very* nice.

She turned suddenly, realising what I was up to, and gave me a knowing smirk.

'What . . .' I sniffed, 'is that incredible smell?'

'Her perfume. Fabulous, isn't it. She only went out a few minutes ago and left a trail of it through the flat. I walk up and down in it until it disappears.'

We broke out into the lounge, furnished wall-to-distant-wall in white curly carpeting deep enough to play hide-and-seek in.

'Oh, my . . .' I exclaimed. 'How incredible – it's *just* like my place. She must go to my interior decorator.'

'I'll bet,' she laughed.

'Frances, isn't it?'

'Yes.'

'Frances what, may I ask?'

'Don't you dare laugh . . . it's Drake. And no cracks about Plymouth Hoe, bowling greens or the Spanish Armada, either.'

'As if I would, though I reckon I owe you something for Randy Comfort. What a super place. She must be doing very well, Miss Suzie Drew.'

In answer she picked up a copy of *Vogue* and flashed the cover at me. 'That well, is all.'

'Oh . . .'

Suzie Drew was a green-eyed blonde of infinite loveliness, a classic beauty with doe-eyes, a thin, straight nose and a mouth men would gladly die for. But totally unreachable.

'What's she like to work for?'

She shrugged. 'Not bad.'

'Oh, dear, that doesn't sound too good. What don't you like about her?'

Another shrug. 'She's very beautiful but she knows it. I dunno, I suppose it's the way all top models and actresses behave. She's got a terrible temper at times. Really let's rip . . . and her language! You should hear her when something goes wrong with a show or a photograph session. She comes bursting through the door, effin' and blindin' . . . throwing things all over the place. Right cow, she can be at times. But then she can also be very nice, too. She gives me lots of presents . . . gloves, scarves, perfume . . .'

She stopped suddenly and looked at me, interestedly. 'When did you start?'

'Friday.'

'D'you like it?'

'Smashing. Who wouldn't like working amongst all this? You do, don't you?'

'Yes,' she said hesitantly. 'Gets a bit boring at times,

though. She's away nearly all day and most week-ends, and when I've cleaned the flat there's not much to do.'

I grinned at her. 'Can't you pretend it's all yours and have a lovely time? You could play records . . . try her clothes on . . . invite a boyfriend in.'

'Not likely,' she laughed. 'Oh, I *do* play records and try her clothes on, but I daren't invite a boyfriend in.'

'Have you got one?'

'Mm . . . sort of. But I can only see him on my day off, I have to be here at nights.'

'Mmmm . . . looks like what you need is a boyfriend right here in the buildings, doesn't it, someone who could pop in from time to time without causing any suspicion.'

She gave me a knowing grin. 'Someone like you, for instance?'

'Well, yes, a chap in my position would do nicely, it seems to me.'

'Are you offering?'

I gave a fatalistic shrug. 'We, the staff, must stick together, Frances.'

'Fran.'

'Fran. Don't you think so? I mean, if we can't help each other in times of hardship . . .'

'I am *not* hard up, Mister Comfort.'

'I'm sure.'

'It's just that . . . it gets a bit lonely from time to time.'

'Of course.'

'And if you *wanted* to pop in now and then for a cup of tea, I'd be very glad to see you.'

'Fine, you're on. You know where I live, just call Jack Berryweed and tell him that . . . well, I'm sure you'll be able to think of something. OK?'

She smiled. 'OK. I'd better show you where that bathroom cabinet is.'

She showed me.

This one was for real. It had brought four big lumps of wall off with it, leaving four good-sized craters.

'Ah . . .' I said.

'Ah, what?' she said, squatting on the side of the bath to watch me.

'This is going to be a two-day job.'

'Really?' she chuckled. 'Two days for *that*?'

'No, *really*. I'll have to fill these holes in and give the plaster time to set – that'll take until tomorrow. I'd better come back Wednesday to screw it back on the wall.'

'All right.'

'Do you think I could borrow a pudding basin or something – to mix the plaster in?'

'Yes, sure, there's one in the kitchen.'

'Fine. Er . . . pop the kettle on while you're there, hey?'

After she'd gone I broke into a little jig. Was there no *end* to the potential of this job!

One thing, though – I'd have to start a diary straight away, or I'd be forgetting appointments and upsetting people. I already had two to remember; five o'clock the next night for Rachel Roget and Wednesday for Fran. I'd get a desk diary on the way to work Tuesday and keep it up from now on, putting in future occasions that might come in handy – like birthdays and things. An unsuspected little present at the right moment might work miracles. Oh, this was going to be done properly or not at all.

She seemed to take rather a long time getting the basin and when she returned she'd combed out her hair and put some lipstick and eye stuff on. She really was quite a little cracker.

'That's nice,' I said, indicating her hair.

'Oh, you noticed.'

'Well, of course. It really suits you like that, but I suppose you've got to wear it up when madam's at home. You've got lovely hair, Fran.'

'It's naturally blonde, not dyed, you know.'

'I can see that.' I gave her a wink and clicked my tongue. 'Bit of a smasher, aren't you.'

'Here . . .' she grinned, handing me the basin. 'Get on with it while I make the tea.'

It took me all of three minutes to make up some Polyfilla and fill the holes, then I went looking for her, finding her in the kitchen. I handed her the basin.

'Ta, love, just give it a swill, it'll come off.'

I took a stool and watched her at the sink, enjoying the sideways shimmy of her neat bottom as she scrubbed out the basin and wondering what she'd do if I crept up behind her and . . .

No rough stuff, the warning voice said. Just play it cool, everything comes to him who waits.

'You live in, do you, Fran?'

'Yes, I've got my own room. Miss Drew often has to get up at five o'clock to go off shooting, so I have to live in.'

'Nice room, is it?'

She turned round, drying the basin, and gave me a tight smile. 'I suppose you'd like to see it.'

'Wouldn't mind. I'd like to see what you've got . . . because I might be living in myself.'

'Really? Where?'

'In one of the wings, don't know which. I put it to Mister Berryweed that it would be better if I was on call at the week-ends and he agreed, said he'd talk to the owners. So, we might be neighbours.'

'Fancy that,' she mocked, moving to the teapot.

'Yes, I do.'

'Milk and sugar?'

'Both, please . . . cigarette?'

She took one, lit it, then she poured the tea and sat down opposite.

'First visitor you've ever had?' I asked.

'To tea, yes.'

'Must be very lonely for you.'

'It is.'

'And Miss Drew sometimes goes away for a whole week-end, hm?'

'Now and then.'

'What happens then, do you still stay here?'

'No, I go home to my Mum's, she lives in Putney.'

'Mmm . . . but you could stay here if you wanted?'

Her smile was downright suspicious. 'And what's going on in *your* mind?'

'Nothing,' I protested with a laugh. 'I just thought . . . if I moved in and there wasn't much doing over a week-end, I might sort of . . . pop-up and see you, that's all.'

'And we'd have this lovely flat to ourselves, you mean?'

'Well, no, I hadn't thought of it like *that*, Fran. I mean, I wouldn't take advantage of your boss's absence or anything . . .'

'Wouldn't you?'

'Certainly not.'

'You mean you wouldn't want to sit out there in the lounge and listen to her records and dance with me and perhaps have a drink or two and . . .'

'Good heavens, no, that wouldn't be fair on her, would it?'

'How could she know if she was in Marbella or the South of France or . . .'

'She might come back unexpectedly and catch us.'

'Oh, so you have thought about it,' she teased.

I laughed. 'Hey, be a bit of a hoot, though, wouldn't it, you and me spending a week-end in a six hundred pound-a-month flat . . . living like lords on our wages.'

'Oh, so now we're spending the week-end together. We seem to have come a long way from having the odd cup of tea in a very short time.'

'Nah, you know what I mean . . .'

'Yes, I do, you'd like to spend the week-end here, is what you mean.'

'Well, you can't blame a fellow for fancying the idea.'

'It'd be more than my job was worth.'

'Oh, certainly . . .'

'The *thought* of her walking in and catching us at it . . . I mean, dancing together.'

'Too horrible to contemplate. Mind you, as you say, it's highly unlikely if she's in Marbella or the South of France . . . but I suppose she *could* come back unexpectedly . . . couldn't she?'

'Yes, she *could* . . . though it hasn't happened in two years. She always calls me from the airport to let me know she's on her way so I can make sure the place is tidy and the hot water's on, that sort of thing.'

'Two years, hm?'

'Yes, two years.'

'Long time. Well, thanks a million for the tea, Fran, I must get cracking, got a busy day today.'

As we reached the hall, she said, 'Would you . . . like to see my room?'

I coughed. 'Yes, I would.'

It was at the end of the corridor – a neat girl's room with a single bed covered by one of those European quilt things that you use instead of conventional bedding.

'Very nice,' I said, conscious of how close she was standing . . . and of the perfume she'd pinched from her boss's bottle. 'Comfy, are they, those quilts?'

'Warm as toast.'

'You smell lovely, Fran.'

'Do I?'

'I'd like to kiss you.'

'Would you now . . . well, you can't. Come on, you have to go.'

She made to push past me. I put my hand out, caught her lightly by the shoulder and swung her towards me, and, by God, next thing we were eating each other.

What a kisser! She was all over me, biting my lips and

stuffing her tongue in my mouth and gasping for breath like she'd just run from Piccadilly Circus.

Well, I mean, that was it. Up came Brutus with one hell of a rush and the thrust of him against her belly sent her into fresh paroxysms of desire. She moaned and groaned and ground her belly so hard against him I feared mortal injury.

Meanwhile, I wasn't just standing there taking notes. Two flicks and a swish and the back of her dress was open to the waist. Hot flesh met my hands and drove me to further exploration . . . down her panties to her wonderful bottom.

'Don't . . .' she gasped, still chewing my lips off.

So I didn't. I withdrew and went up the front instead . . . down the front of her panties and into the hot, moist recess between her thighs.

'No . . . no . . .' she was protesting, opening wide so I could get right up there. God, she was lovely.

'On the bed!' I whispered.

'No, not that . . . not this time.'

'What, then?'

'Just this . . . oh, that's wonderful . . . oh!' Her eyes flew wide. 'I think I'm coming!'

'Really?'

'Ohh . . . ohhhh . . .!' she cried, then suddenly her arms snapped round me like bands of steel, her thighs slapped together on my hand, and she went into a knee-buckled slump and thrust hard . . . twice . . . three times against my arm, bringing herself off a treat.

'Ohhhh . . .!' she gasped and fell against me.

'There, there . . .' I chuckled, stroking her hair, giving her a hug. 'That was a little beauty, wasn't it.'

She looked up at me, smiling bashfully, tears moistening her eyes. 'Aren't I awful . . . you'll hate me.'

'I'll what?' I laughed. 'Honey, you don't know your Uncle Randy. I'm delighted . . . I think it was lovely.'

'Really? But you didn't . . . you know.'

I kissed her soft, pliant mouth. 'My turn will come.'

'Will you come back?'

'Try and stop me.'

She hugged me nicely.

'I think you needed that,' I observed.

She nodded against my chest. 'I've been so lonely . . .'

'Well, not anymore. Come here, let me do your zip up.'

I turned her round and got her straightened out, then turned her again and kissed her, holding her face. 'You all right?'

She beamed a smile.

'Good girl.'

Her smile faded. 'Are *you* all right?'

I looked down and coughed. 'Well, I shall probably suffer agony all day with lover's nuts, but not to worry . . .'

'I'm sorry. I just felt . . . well, I wasn't quite ready.'

'Sweetheart . . .' I kissed her on the nose, '. . . tomorrow is another day – and so is the day after. It'll happen when it happens, so long as you want it to happen.'

'You're very nice.'

'See you Wednesday?'

'See you Wednesday.'

She blew me a kiss from the apartment door and I blew one back and went down the stairs, chuckling.

CHAPTER SEVEN

The day slipped by quickly, quietly, and, excitement-wise, uneventfully after my little tete-a-tete with Fran. There was plenty to do but nothing developed during the calls. As a matter of fact, accompanied by Jack Berryweed, I worked on three unoccupied apartments, the residents being out all day.

This, understandably, was the rule, that Jack supervised my work on unoccupied flats, and it was, as he explained, as much for my own protection as protection of the property. There was a wealth of stuff in these places and if anything was claimed to be missing, the suspicion would naturally fall on me. So I was more than happy with the arrangement.

Apart from that, it gave him a chance to see me working and to put his mind at ease that I was doing the jobs properly; and it gave me a chance, in the course of casual conversation, to find out a bit more about the residents concerned, the information going straight into my memory bank for future use.

We got back to his office about half four, just in time for tea (which he insisted I make), and we were sitting there having a quiet cuppa, believing that was it for the day, when the phone rang.

'Porter's Lodge,' he announced. 'Ah, yes, Mrs Erm . . . oh, really . . . yes, well you're in luck, you just caught him . . . five o'clock, madam . . . no, I'm sure he won't mind, he's a very willing lad. He'll be over directly. Thank you, madam.'

He put the receiver down and pulled out his watch. 'Blimey, it's ten to.' He regarded me over his specs. 'Mind a bit of unpaid overtime, Randy? Lady in Three is in a spot of trouble – she's gorn and blocked her sink up with potting clay . . .'

Number Three! Mrs Dexter! Ha!

'No, I don't mind, Mr Berryweed. What's the lady's name?'

'Mrs Dexter. Very nice. Her husband's something big in the city, when he's at home, that is. Spends 'alf his time in Switzerland with the gnomes of Zurich. Shouldn't take you long, should it?'

'Probably not, but I'll go straight home from her place, if you don't mind. I'm going to the pictures tonight. I'll just take a wrench and a screwdriver, that's all I'll need.'

'You're a good lad. Don't think it isn't appreciated.'

'Nah, what's a couple of minutes overtime, for heaven's sake. Well, I'll be off. See you tomorrow.'

I had to control the urge to break into a gallop. With thumping heart I crossed over to the West Wing and walked down the corridor, pausing to collect myself before ringing the bell.

The door opened immediately, as though she'd been waiting at it.

Boy, what a transformation. Gone was the pottery smock, the smudged nose and the unkempt auburn hair. She now looked quite ravishing in a knee-length dress of apple-green silk that clung to her body like a second skin, emphasising this and that and framing a picture of mature womanhood that was altogether extremely haveable.

'Hello,' she said, her wide mouth curving in an enticing smile. 'I do apologise for calling so late. I didn't realise you went home at five.'

'No trouble at all, Mrs Dexter. I'm in no hurry.'

'Won't you come in.'

The place was spotless. I expected to see traces of hobby clutter but there wasn't a painting easel or pottery wheel in sight. I followed her through the lounge into the kitchen, done in olive green and white, the walls decorated with ceramic tiles that had cost somebody a fortune.

'Very stupid of me,' she admitted. 'I poured some runny

clay down the sink, thinking it would wash away, but I'm afraid I've blocked the pipe.'

'No problem, Mrs Dexter. It's probably just settled in the U-bend. We'll have it clear in no time.'

'Are you sure I'm not keeping you? Surely you like to leave on time . . . you must have things to do.'

'No, nothing much. I was thinking of going to the pictures, but I can go another night.'

'Oh, you were . . . going by yourself? You won't be letting anyone else down?'

Subtle, that. My marital/romantic status established right off.

'No, I'm a bachelor gay,' I grinned. 'I travel light . . . master of my own destiny.'

'Very sensible,' she agreed readily. 'At your age. But how about your family? Won't you be expected for dinner?'

Ho ho, no messing about with this one.

'I don't live with my parents, Mrs Dexter. I have a room in a boarding house not far from here and I come and go as I please. I can eat dinner any old time.'

'A truly free man. I admire your spirit of independence.'

And that wasn't all she was admiring by the way her eyes were flicking here and there and back again.

'But surely *I'm* keeping *you*,' I said, playing her little game. 'You must be waiting to go out.'

'No,' she said lightly. 'Why, do I look as though I'm waiting to go out?'

I grinned deferentially. 'Well, excuse me for saying so, but yes, you do. You look so . . . no, I shouldn't say it, it's very personal.'

'Go on,' she laughed, obviously delighted with our rapport. 'I look so what? Tell me, I won't mind.'

'Well . . . so nice. You look dressed for town.'

'I do?' she laughed, inspecting herself as though she didn't know what she was wearing. 'Well, thank you, but it's just an ordinary dress . . .'

'It's very lovely, Mrs Dexter. The colour suits you.'

'Well, thank you.' She smiled demurely, quite overcome, and I reckoned that was enough of the old horse to be going on with.

I turned my attention to the sink. 'I wonder if I could borrow a bucket, Mrs Dexter? When I unscrew the trap, the clay will pour out and we need to catch it in something.'

'Yes, certainly.'

She went to a cupboard and brought back a plastic bucket. 'How's this?'

'That'll do fine.'

I crouched down, opened the low cupboard under the sink, removed a few things from it, then sprawled out on the floor and lay with my head and shoulders under the trap.

From this position I could see only her lower half, from her thighs down, and took the opportunity to have a good look at her legs. They were very good – slender, well-shaped thighs and calves, whittling down to well-turned ankles and neat, small feet. She may have been knocking forty but she was in damn good shape. Probably no kids.

But while I was surreptitiously ogling *her* lower half, I could tell from the angle at which she was standing that she was ogling mine! I mean, that's all there was of me to see.

Right, I thought, if that's what you want, love, that's what you'll get. So, reaching for my wrench, I clamped it on the trap nut and went into a performance of grunting and straining that would've got me an Oscar any day of the week, each spasm of effort accompanied by a wide-spread thrashing of the limbs and an arching of the pelvic region that must have brought The Brute out in sharp relief and had her eyes popping out of their sockets.

'By . . . heaven, this is stiff,' I gasped.

'Oh, dear . . . do you think you'll be able to do it?'

'It'll come in a minute, Mrs Dexter, it's purely a battle of wills.'

'Can I help in any way?'

Yes, sit on this and keep my thighs down, I was dying to suggest.

'No, thank you, ma'm . . . ' I risked a little joke. 'It's a bit of a squeeze under here for two.'

Her laughter told me she enjoyed it.

'Oh . . . *boy* . . .' I grunted, getting another good arch in and really spreading them this time. 'I doubt if this has been off since the apartments were built.'

'I'm so sorry you're having so much trouble.'

'No trouble at all. All in a day's work . . . ah! here she comes!'

'Oh, good.'

I shifted to one side and got the bucket under the trap, then unscrewed the plug all the way, expecting a bit of an avalanche. But nothing happened. I went up the hole with the screwdriver and hit something hard, gave the driver a couple of twists and brought it down. It was covered with solid clay!

So, me beauty, you told Randy a fib. This was no runny clay you poured in here – you broke off little bits and shoved it down the hole until it was blocked, you naughty, conniving, sexually frustrated, adorably wanton lady.

'Boy, it really is blocked,' I commented. 'But you aren't the culprit, Mrs Dexter, somebody got here before you. You might have brought things to a head a little, but it would've choked sooner or later.'

'Oh . . .' she said, as though pleased I thought so. 'Can you unblock it?'

'Yes, it's coming slowly . . . perhaps a little water might help. Could you turn the tap on a trickle, please – cold water.'

'Yes, certainly.'

She came closer, having to open her legs to straddle one of mine. I couldn't see too far up but the sight of the inside of her thigh just above the knee got my heart thumping again and the temptation to plunge my hand up was almost irresistible. Fortunately the cold water came down at that moment and ran up my arm into my shirt, quenching my ardour.

'Aggh!' I gasped, then laughed.

'What's the matter?'

'Got a shirtful of cold water, that's all.'

'Oh, dear, you'll be soaked.'

'All part of the job, Mrs Dexter – and a little cold water never hurt anybody,' I said, purposely smearing some runny clay over my face, arms, chest and shirt. Nothing like it for evoking feminine sympathy.

'Ah, it's coming away, now . . . lovely . . . come on, my beauty . . .' Poking away with the screwdriver I got a nice flow running and in a few minutes clear water was pouring through. 'Right, you can turn off now, please, Mrs Dexter. I'll screw the plug back and we'll give it a try.'

'Wonderful!' She made it sound like we'd just conquered Everest together.

'Right . . . fire away!'

On came the taps.

'You did it! Oh, well done . . . well done.'

Puffing and panting a bit I crawled out of the cupboard, collected the bucket and tools and stood up, giving my face a final wipe with my muddy arm to make sure I looked a mess.

'Oh . . .!' Her mouth popped open. 'Oh, dear, you *have* been suffering under there.'

'It's only mud, Mrs Dexter. A little bit of *that* never hurt anybody either. It'll wash off easy enough.'

'But your shirt! You really can't go home looking like that, we must do something.' She pretended to think, then suddenly had the solution. 'Look, take it off and I'll put it through the washing machine, it'll be washed and dried in half an hour . . . if you can stay that long, that is.'

'Well, yes, I could, but . . . oh, you don't want to be bothered doing that.'

'Nonsense. You were good enough to work after hours for me, it's the least I can do. Come on, off with it . . . and while it's washing, I think the best place for you is the bath, young man!'

Tee-*rum*-tee-dum-dee-dum.

I met the suggestion with an amused, startled expression, giving her her lead.

'No, I insist. Good gracious, it's all over your chest. You've got so many places to wash, you may as well have a bath. Come on, give me the shirt . . .'

With a resigned sigh, I peeled it off, making a good show of bracing arm and chest muscles which by no means was lost on her, and handed her the shirt. 'Well, this is very good of you . . .'

'I'm enjoying it,' she laughed. 'I haven't had so much fun in months. Come on, I'll show you the bathroom.'

It was, of course, another splendid lay-out, in browns, yellows and greens, the bath itself a miniature mosaic-ed swimming pool, much like Nicopopolous's.

'Wow,' I gasped admiringly, as though I'd never seen a place like it before. 'Now, this is what I call a bathroom. And the bath! It's big enough for four people!'

'Though not its customary role,' she grinned. 'Well, there you are, help yourself. Come through when you're finished.'

I shook my head. 'I can't believe it – all this to myself. It's not much like Mrs Maloney's bathroom, I can tell you, she's my landlady. Her bath's so small I can't lie down in it . . . I have to wash in stages.'

'I would have thought you'd have trouble in most normal baths. You're a very big . . . you're very tall. What are you smiling at?'

I pulled my nose. 'I was just wondering what your husband would say if he came in and found a strange man in his tub. It would take some explaining, wouldn't it?'

'No. I would simply tell him the truth and that would be that.'

I laughed. 'You must have a very understanding husband, Mrs Dexter.'

'Well, let's say that at the moment I have a very *distant* one, so the problem will not arise.'

'Oh, away, is he?'

'He's in Kenya . . . fishing.'

'My, that is distant.'

'Yes . . . well, there you are, help yourself to anything you want. I'll get on with the shirt.'

'Thank you very much, Mrs Dexter.'

She exited, leaving the door ajar. Whether it was intentional or not, I don't know, but I left it ajar, crossed to the bath, yanked down two gilt handles and was soon lost in a cloud of steam. Five minutes later I was wallowing in scented luxury, the like of which I would never have believed available to Randolph Turpin Comfort.

Floating in a sea of soft, velvety suds, I gazed about and marvelled that I was there, little old me from nowhere, luxuriating in all this wealth and splendour. But how well it suited my metabolism. I really felt quite at home.

Yes, I could see me living in an apartment like this, with a maid like Fran to pamper my momentary desire. Fran, love, in you pop and scrub my back . . . now my front. Good girl, now into bed and warm the sheets, I'll be there in a minute.

I smiled to myself at the thought of it, realising I was as good as there already. If I played my cards right I *could* practically live in a place like this, or several places like it. A night here . . . a weekend there. Better than having your own place, really, and there'd be the additional benefit of variety. You wouldn't get fed up with the decor so quickly.

One last swish across the pool and it was time to get out. I didn't want to overdo it.

I pulled the lever that operated the huge plug and as the sudsy water ran out, I turned on the taps and gave myself a fresh sluice. Then I was out and drying myself on a big, fluffy yellow towel.

It was during one of my back-drying contortions that I caught a glimpse of Mrs Dexter in one of the big mirrors that fronted a line of cupboards. She was out in the hall, round the corner out of direct sight, but was picking my reflection up very nicely in the mirrors.

My pulse erupted, but I managed to avoid her gaze and continued drying myself as though I'd seen nothing.

Had she, I wondered, purposely left the door ajar? If so, she must have put two and two together and realised I had *also* purposely left it open, inviting her to take a butcher's. And that being so, the game was surely afoot!

Right, love, if an eyeful is what your little heart desires, it's what it'll get. But first a little tease to get you on the boil.

For three or four minutes I rubbed here, I rubbed there, always keeping the towel covering the important parts. She must have been going potty, wondering when the curtain was going to drop. Lousy trick, really. I could imagine how I'd be feeling if the roles were reversed. I'd be gnashing my teeth with angst.

Well, enough was enough, so I edged towards the mirrors to make sure she'd have a good close-up view, then suddenly abandoned the towel altogether and went into a series of exercises, stretching up high and out wide, deep breathing to fill my chest, sideways bending, arms flinging sideways, until I reckoned she was up around four hundred Centigrade, then I put my clothes on.

When I reached the hall she was, of course, long gone. I went through and found her in the kitchen, standing guard over the washing machine.

'Ah, there you are,' she smiled, looking flushed I thought. 'Did you enjoy your bath?'

'Wonderful. You must have heard me singing from here.'

'No, it's quite a distance from here. If you'd told me you were going to sing, I'd have listened outside the door.'

The cheeky madam.

'Oh, you didn't miss much,' I said.

And *that* was no lie.

'Perhaps you're too modest, Randy.'

There, I'd been waiting for my name, feeling that the mention of it might well signify an important step forward in our blossoming relationship. 'No, singing is not one of the things I do well, Mrs Dexter.'

'Oh? What *are* the things you do well?'

Birds like you, love. You scheming monkey, how can you stand there looking so damned innocent when you purposely blocked the sink and have just been ogling me in the nod.

'Not much,' I smiled, self-effacingly. 'Jack of all trades and master of none, that's me.'

'I somehow doubt that's true. I'm sure there are some things you do supremely well. To me you have an artistic mien . . . a splended sensitivity. I don't think it's possible for a man with these qualities to be totally unaccomplished.'

'Well, that's very nice of you, Mrs Dexter, but I can't think of anything that I'm terrific at right now, unless you count an appreciation of your company and your kindness.'

'There,' she laughed, 'you've just demonstrated a great talent, a talent for saying the right thing. You've no idea how much a woman appreciates compliments like that.'

How wrong you are, love.

'Oh,' I smiled, 'that requires no effort. I just said what I felt.'

'How very sweet. I really do feel you've missed your vocation, Randy . . . you should have been a diplomat, or better still a screen lover. You'd have women swooning in the aisles.'

'Really?' I laughed.

'But indeed. There is so little romance in life these days and we women miss it terribly. It does our hearts good to receive compliments, sweet nothings, from a gentle, sensitive man. We need to be swept off our feet with a little smooth talk and carried into our boudoirs in the arms of romance – figuratively speaking, of course . . . unless one is fortunate to be blessed with a husband who possesses such qualities, and then there would be no need to speak figuratively!' she laughed.

'*Are* you blessed with one, Mrs Dexter?'

She faltered. 'I . . .'

'I'm sorry, that's a very personal question, I shouldn't have asked it.'

She smiled, wanly. 'My dear Randy, I don't mind, it was a natural question to ask and . . . I don't mind in the least answering. It does one good to talk at times . . . particularly to such an understanding person as yourself.'

'We all need someone to talk to at times, Mrs Dexter. I imagine being here by yourself so much is a bit of a strain, isn't it. Even amongst all this luxury I imagine you feel pretty frus . . . pretty lonely at times.'

'Indeed I do. Charles is a wonderful husband, Randy, terribly kind and generous, but he's away such an awful lot on business.'

'Oh, he's in Kenya on business? Sorry, I thought you said he was fishing.'

'Yes, he is, but . . . well, it's sort of mixed with business, you understand.'

Yes, monkey business, I thought. Old Charlie had just pushed off on holiday on his tod!

'I couldn't possibly have gone along,' she insisted, perhaps reading my mind. 'For one thing, battling with enormous whale-like creatures on the end of a rod is *not* my idea of a holiday.'

'And what is your idea of a holiday, Mrs Dexter?'

She waxed romantic, gazed at the ceiling with a far-way look in her eyes. 'Oh . . . lying on white sand in the Bahamas . . . sailing the blue Caribbean . . . dancing under the stars in St. Tropez . . .'

'With a tall, dark, handsome Frenchman, I take it?'

'If possible, yes!' she laughed, her eyes now, for the first time, beginning to play games, to exchange intimacies with mine. 'What I mean is . . . Charles doesn't dance. And I'm afraid I love to dance. Do you dance, Randy?'

Yeh, yeh, yeh!

'A little,' I admitted.

'There you go again, being modest, I'm sure. I'm certain you dance extremely well, you have the build for it.'

'Well, let's say I can hold a rhythm.'

'Yes . . . I'm sure you can.' Her eyes dropped to my naked chest, then went to the washing machine. 'Randy, you can't possibly wear this for ages yet. Come . . . let's find you something else to wear. Charles has hundreds of shirts he's never worn. I'm sure we can fit you with something. Come into the bedroom.'

The bedroom, in keeping with local tradition, was palatial. The floor smothered in blue Chinese carpet, the bed a vast acreage of pale blue satin, and the wardrobes a thirty-foot run of white louvred cupboards.

She opened three, flung them wide, revealing a stock not far short of Simpson's.

'Look, dozens of them. Try something on that shelf.'

I took a couple of shirts, brand new, still in their cellophane wrappers, removed one in navy silk and slipped it on, my neck hairs bristling to its sensuous caress.

'Oh, boy . . .'

'You like that one? It looks awfully good on you.'

'I love it.'

'It's yours. Charles doesn't know to the nearest fifty how many he's got. He's probably had that two or three years. Does that other one please you? Have that one, too.'

'Oh, Mrs Dexter, I couldn't . . .'

'You could and you will, Randy. It gives me a great deal more pleasure seeing you wearing it than keeping the shelf warm. Take them . . . for being so nice.'

'Well, thank you very much. They're very beautiful.'

She smiled as she closed the doors. 'Come . . . let's have a drink while your shirt's drying. Would you like a drink?'

'Yes, thank you.'

'It's six o'clock, the sun's down over the yard-arm, and our consciences are clear,' she laughed. 'So, let's go and splice the main-brace.'

In the lounge she directed me to sit on a long, pale-pink silk-covered sofa and went to an antique cupboard to fix the drinks.

'What would you like . . . scotch?'

'What's your favourite?'

'Oh, I usually have a gin and tonic this time of night.'

'Then I'll have one, too.'

She brought them over in crystal glasses that looked too fragile to hold.

'You have some beautiful things, Mrs Dexter,' I said, looking down her dress as she placed the drinks on the table.

'You enjoy beautiful things, Randy, don't you?'

'Very much.'

'So do I. But how much nicer when you can share their pleasure with someone who also appreciates them.'

She re-crossed the room to an antique stereogram and in a moment flooded the room with quiet, romantic orchestral music, then returned.

'That suit?'

'It's lovely.'

She dropped to the sofa, curling one leg under her and faced me, reached for her drink and raised a toast.

'To beautiful things.'

'To you, Mrs Dexter.'

Her eyes touched mine over the glass, telling me the compliment had gone home. She put down the glass and offered me a cigarette from a silver box. I took one, lit hers with the silver table lighter, then my own and exhaled thoughtfully.

'You have so many beautiful things to drink to, haven't you, Mrs Dexter?'

She nodded. 'Yes. And yet it takes someone like you to remind me how much I have got. It's a terrible thing to admit, perhaps, but there are times when I really do lose sight of just how beautiful these . . . possessions are.'

'Why shouldn't you? You can't spend your life staring in awe at a sofa, as magnificent as this one is. There are other things far more important.'

Her brow furrowed. 'How right you are, Randy. My, you *are* good for my ego.'

I shrugged. 'You've got life in proper perspective, people first, possessions second.'

She laughed delightedly. 'Randy, I told you you were hiding your light under a bushel. You're a natural-born philosopher. Tell me about yourself.'

'Oh, no, Mrs Dexter. I'm not going to bore you with life in a South Wimbledon semi. I'd rather talk about more exciting things, you, for instance.'

'Me!' she laughed, throwing up her head. 'My dear, you'd have to look very hard to find anyone *less* exciting.'

I gave her the eyes, direct and earnest. 'I don't think so.'

She faltered. 'I . . . oh, *no*, Randy! I live the most unadventurous existence. I belong to clubs I never go to because they're full of women like me . . . I potter around at silly hobbies pretending I'm being frightfully creative . . .'

'Perhaps all you need . . . is someone to be exciting *with*?'

That stopped her.

She looked at me strangely, breathlessly, her flippancy gone. For a moment she maintained her searching gaze, her eyes fixed on mine, then, with a mock-prim smile, she broke the spell and turned away to pick up her glass.

'What *are* you suggesting, Randy Comfort?'

'Perhaps I'm over-reaching myself, Mrs Dexter. I'm sorry.'

'Don't be silly. Randy, this is after-hours . . . and you're not the sort of man to take advantage. If you were, you wouldn't be sitting here now. Please . . . say what you like . . . and *do* what you like, I shan't be offended. I value your company. To tell the truth . . . I'm extremely glad you were able to stay. I was feeling particularly down tonight.' She gave a shrug and a quick smile. 'Kenya blues, I suppose . . . following on Switzerland blues and New York blues and so many other blues.'

She looked up at me, earnestly. 'Randy, I want you to forget our relative positions . . . at least for tonight, do you understand? I want us to have some *fun*.' She laughed and nodded at my glass. 'Come on, drink up, I feel like letting my hair down. It's been so long since I kicked off my shoes and got a bit tiddly, that's *precisely* what I'm going to do! Are you game?'

'Yes,' I laughed, 'I'm game.'

'Splendid. I knew I could count on you. Well . . . here's to *all* beautiful things . . . and may we share one or two together.'

And with that she drained her glass.

'Ooh!' she gasped. 'Come on, bottoms up! You're not going to stay cold, stone sober.'

Zonk!

Down mine went.

She stood up, kicked both shoes across the room, picked up my glass and waltzed back to the bar, singing to the orchestra. '*I* feel like a party, just the two of us, what d'you say?'

'Proposal unanimously carried, Mrs Dexter.'

'You're a sport. Come and show me how you can't dance.'

There is simply *nothing* like dancing to get things going. After all, what is it but, as the song says, making love set to music?

At first she kept it lively, jovial, jocular, talking a blue streak as the gin began its insidious annihilation of her reserve. But gradually, as record followed record, she became more and more amorous, more flirtatious, cuddling close, cheek to cheek, hugging me tight and making it perfectly plain she'd locked out all her inhibitions for the evening and thrown away the key.

'You *do* dance divinely,' she cooed, her lips nibbling my cheek, both arms round my neck and her belly pressed to mine.

'This is dancing?' I grinned.

'Randy . . . do you day-dream?'

'All the time.'

'So do I. I have the most wicked fantasies about a tall, dark, handsome young man who calls now and then to relieve my boredom.'

'And what do you do together . . . in your fantasies?'

'At first we just talk, everything very circumspect . . . then I see he's looking at me in a certain way. His eyes undress me . . . and what he sees, he likes, just as you did, you naughty boy.'

I chuckled an admission.

'Then we have a drink or two . . . put on some music . . . dance . . .'

I was trembling now, knowing things were coming to the boil. My throat was tight and a nervous tick fluttered in my cheek. 'Yes? . . . And what then?'

'Then, suddenly . . . he kisses me.'

I gulped. 'Like this?'

She raised her face, wanting it. Our mouths met. We tasted each other, then passion exploded and we were into it, ferociously. She groaned hungrily, thrust into me, her fingers raking my neck.

'Yes, yes,' she whispered tremulously. '*Just* like that.'

'And then?' I croaked.

'Then . . . he takes me by the hand and leads me into the bedroom . . . and I follow, willingly . . .'

'Like this?'

When we reached the bedroom, she closed the heavy

drapes, put on a soft bed-side light and returned to me, smiling. 'It's phenomenal . . . this is precisely how I imagined it.'

'And what happens next?'

'Then . . . he undresses me.'

'Like this?'

A quick zip and her little dress lay at her feet. Two hooks unhooked and her bra fell away, revealing full, beautiful breasts, hard, excited nipples. My heart was thudding so hard I could scarcely breathe.

I dropped to my knees, hooked my thumbs into the waist of her little green panties and drew them down, exploding with excitement as her thick, auburn cluster was revealed.

A moment later she stood naked as born.

I threw my arms around her and pressed my lips to her warm belly, rained kisses upon it and all around it, knowing from her fingers driving through my hair that it was exactly what she wanted.

She uttered a delicious groan and raised my face to hers. 'Stand up,' she murmured.

I stood. Off came the shirt. My trousers opened, dropped. I kicked them aside with my shoes. Now she fell to her knees, likewise hooked fingers into my shorts and slowly drew them down, gasping as my old mate twanged out of confinement like a butcher's knife stuck in a door.

In haste now she got rid of all offending garments, threw them aside, then returned her attention to The Brute, murmuring little maternal mewing sounds of adoration, 'Oh . . . Randy,' gently took him into her hands and kissed him.

'Still as you imagined?' I hoarsed, choked to the gills.

'*Exactly* . . . it couldn't be more precise.'

'And now what happens?'

'This . . .'

With all the sensuous yearning of an ice-cream gormet, she opened her mouth wide and fed him in, wrapped him lovingly in the warm, wet cocoon of her silky tongue and enfolding lips, then proceeded to encircle his throbbing head with a slow deliberate circumnavigation of her tantalising tongue, murmuring softly, eyes closed, lost in ecstacy.

Now she withdrew, placed him against her cheek and raised her eyes to mine in a tender smile. 'He's beautiful, Randy . . . so strong and hard and upright.'

I took hold of her shoulders and drew her to her feet, thrust him between her thighs and held her close. 'He thinks very highly of you, too. What would you like me to do to you, Mrs Dexter? Name it and it's yours.'

'Everything,' she sighed. 'Play with me . . . a nice, long, leisurely game. I don't want it to end too soon.'

'No, of course not. Shall I bring the drinks in?'

Her eyes lit up. 'Yes! We will continue our party right here.'

When I returned with the drinks she was lying on the satin coverlet of the bed, legs slightly parted, gazing with a rapturous smile at the ceiling. 'Know what I've been thinking? I've been thinking how fortunate I am that you came to work here . . . that you conform so precisely to my image of a fantasy lover. You are kind, gentle, experienced, uninhibited, tall, dark and *very* handsome . . . and, also, I know, discreet.' She turned to face me. 'You are discreet, aren't you, Randy?'

'Totally, Mrs Dexter . . . a mute.'

'Splendid. Discretion, you know, apart from being the better part of valour, will bring its own reward.'

'I'm being amply rewarded now, Mrs Dexter.'

'How kind you are. But I have other, more tangible recompense in mind. I would like to share some of my *worldly* wealth with you – as well as my aesthetic treasure.'

Whee hee!

'You're very kind, Mrs Dexter,' I smiled, handing her her drink.

She sat up and took a gulp, regarding me smokily over the rim. 'How very relaxed you are . . . and how very beautiful. I can scarcely believe my good fortune.'

'Nor I mine.'

'Oh, come, now, finding girls is not your problem.'

'Finding the right one is. It's not easy to enjoy this without complications.'

'True. In that case, this is a very happy arrangement for both of us, isn't it?'

'Delightful.'

She sprawled across the bed, placed her glass on the side table, then rolled onto her back and beckoned me to join her. 'Come, Randy, delight me . . . play with me . . . do what you will. Feed my fantasy to the full. Give vent to your imagination, your passion . . . your own unbridled fantasies. I promise I shall not be shocked.'

Oh, brother . . .

Well, Comfort, I thought, your hour has come. Play it right and you could tip-toe through clover the rest of your life. The bird's kinky for games, so get out your compendium and sink a shaft into this vast, untapped source of limitless opportunity.

'Right,' I said, narrowing my eyes with mock threat. 'You asked for it, Mrs Dexter.'

I placed my drink on the side table and began to crawl towards her across the bed, evoking an excited chuckle from her with my threatening approach.

'What are you going to do?' she laughed.

'For a start . . . this.'

I fell forward and took her right nipple in my mouth, drawing from her a gasp of surprise and pleasure. 'Oh, Randy . . .'

Suddenly I switched to her left breast, then to her stomach, then back again to her breast . . . kiss, kiss, kiss . . . suck, suck, suck . . . then with a leap I was down the bed and between her legs, and as I struck home with my probing tongue she went through the roof.

'*Randy* . . .!'

Her arms fell sideways, fingers clawing the counterpane, hips arching to meet me. She began to ride, thrust, groan . . .

faster, faster, faster, using me as a rubbing post. Now a low, spiralling moan broke from her . . . she tossed her head, anguished, thrust harder, harder . . . now cried out, 'Randy, I'm coming . . . I'm COMING . . . OHHHHHH! . . .' and 'OHHHHHH!' again, big, bellowing shouts that filled the room, and still she thrust, jerked, pushed . . . now shuddered, in concert with a huge, final bellow, then collapsed, and lay there ohhh-ing and ahhh-ing, her face contorted in a laughing snarl of tortured sensitivity, 'Oh, Randy . . . Randy . . .'

'You liked that? Then I shall do it again.'

'Oh, no . . .'

'Oh, yes.'

In I went, a gossamer caress, and she put up no resistance. A moment more and she had collected herself, became still with renewed concentration. 'Ohhh . . .' A sigh. 'Oh, Randy, that is beautiful . . . you'll make me come again, you naughty boy . . .'

I said nothing, just kept on, a fleeting, feather-like stroke . . . up and up . . . and up . . .

'Oh, God . . .' She threw her head, gasped, began once more to follow my rhythm, up . . . and up . . . and up . . . 'You devil, you're doing it to me again . . . Randy, I've never come twice so quickly before . . . ohhh . . . ohhhh . . . *ohhhh.*'

Now she was into the big time . . . arching off the bed as thought it was red hot, driving into me, bucking, rutting . . . faster and faster . . . nails ravaging the counterpane . . . teeth bared, eyes clamped tight, then . . . 'OHHHHHHH! OH, MY GOD . . . OHHHHHHH!' And she was over the fence once more, bellowing her achievement to the world, finalizing the matter with a deafening roar before collapsing, floppily, in a heap.

'Ohhhh . . .' she groaned, shaking her head. 'You *awful* man . . . you awful, lovely, gorgeous, rude, delicious man . . . come up here and be reprimanded.'

I lay alongside her, my arms around her, her cheek on my chest.

'Where *did* you learn to do that?' she murmured exhaustedly.

'It's the first time I've done it,' I lied. 'You spurred my imagination.'

She gave a delighted chuckle. 'Honestly?'

'It takes two to tango, Mrs Dexter. A man has to know he's on receptive ground before he chances a thing like that. A rebuff could set his development as a lover back permanently . . . do it incalculable harm. It's your approach that inspired inventiveness.'

'Really?' she laughed. 'Well, I'm delighted. I wouldn't have missed that for the world.'

'Was that true, that you've never come twice so quickly?'

'Randy, I rarely get the opportunity to come twice at all. My husband is not, unfortunately, as patient nor as wonderfully controlled as you.' She sighed wistfully. 'To tell the truth, he usually comes as soon as he enters me . . . and very often I don't come at all.'

'Oh, that's rotten. I'm beginning to understand why you're so unhappy, him being away so much *and* not satisfying you even when he's at home. Well, never mind, we'll have to try and make up for it, won't we? Perhaps a little session like this every now and again will bring the roses back into your cheeks.'

'Indeed it would. If I felt I could rely on you to . . . pay me a little visit whenever I'm feeling down, I'm sure life here would be so much more bearable.'

'Of course you can rely on me, Mrs Dexter. Matter of fact, I'm hoping to be able to move into a room in the mansions – one like the porter has. He's going to speak to the owners about it. I suggested it might be a good thing to have a maintenance man on duty over the weekends, you know, to take care of any emergency jobs that might crop up, like . . .'

'Like me feeling blue?' she laughed.

'Like Mrs Dexter feeling blue . . . and he thought it was a good idea.'

'*I* think it's a marvellous idea, Randy . . . then you'd be on hand any hour of the day or night, wouldn't you?'

'Day or night.'

'So, if I woke up in the middle of the night, feeling particularly lonely, all I'd have to do is . . .'

'Phone for room service,' I laughed.

She gave me a big hug. 'What a *wonderful* idea . . . and we shall have to see to it that you *do* get a room here. If the owners do object, *I* shall vetoe it. I have many friends in the Mansions and I shall get up a petition, saying we *insist* on a resident maintenance man. You will get your room.'

'Well, we'll see how it goes. If I have any trouble, I'll let you know, shall I?'

'Certainly,' she said, but she wasn't thinking about that now. She had fully recovered and was beginning to think about other things.

'He's very beautiful,' she whispered, sliding her hand down my stomach to grasp The Brute who'd been having a little doze and was lying all thick and flacid, waiting for the chat to stop.

'How lovely he feels like this . . . all spongey and squeezy. I think I'd like to eat him.'

Down she went and in he went, into the cauldron of her mouth, the wet tickly heat of it inflating him to throbbing hardness in seconds.

'That didn't take long,' she laughed, stroking him gently from base to apex. 'What wonderous things they are. Randy . . I want him inside me.'

'Climb aboard, Mrs Dexter.'

She was up and over in an instant, lowering herself onto him effortlessly, sighing wistfully as she came to rest hard against my thighs.

'Comfy?' I grinned.

'Ecstatically.'

'Care for a drink?'

'Mm,' she nodded.

I passed her her glass and she sipped it thoughtfully, smiling down at me, her smile conveying wonderment, disbelief. 'Randy, you *are* an angel,' she sighed. 'I haven't had so much fun as this in years . . . if ever. I can't tell you how much I'm enjoying it . . . how marvellous I feel . . and how much good you've done my ego I was beginning to feel I'd lost all my attraction.'

'Ridiculous. You're a very sexy-looking woman. I thought so when I first spoke to you.'

'I know you did, I saw it in your eyes. You've no idea how long the week-end seemed, waiting to get you up here. Perhaps I shouldn't be telling you, but your visit *was* contrived, you know. I blocked the sink purposely.'

'I know,' I laughed.

'And I knew you knew . . .but I didn't care. I'd made up my mind to seduce you and I didn't care if it was obvious. My only fear was that you'd refuse . . . that you'd be married or prudish or just not fancy me as much as I thought you did, but I had to take the chance. And I'm very glad I did.'

'So am I, Mrs Dexter.'

'You feel awfully good up here inside me, Randy . . . and I'm getting excited again. I can feel it coming on.'

'Wonderful.'

'Oh, Randy . . . here, take my glass . . .'

I took it and disposed of it.

'*Oh*! that feels good . . .' She raised herself up and lowered again . . . now repeated . . . now faster . . . her face twisting with growing torment. 'Oh, Randy, that is *gorgeous* . . . ohhh . . . ohhh . . .'

She fell forward, supporting herself on my chest. I reached up, took both nipples between thumbs and forefingers to help her on.

'Oh, Randy, that's wonderful!' she cried plaintively, now breaking into a gallop . . . up . . . down . . . up . . . down

. . . up . . . down . . . 'Oh, Lord, I'm coming again . . . I'm coming, Randy . . . OHHHHHHH!'

Once more she bellowed out her triumph, hung high above me and shuddered as the spasms ripped through her, then collapsed in stages with a sob . . . a sob . . . until she was lying down upon my chest. 'Gorgeous . . . gorgeous . . . gorgeous!' she cried, kissing my chest, my neck, my shoulder. 'But, Randy . . .'

'Yes, Mrs Dexter?'

'I want you again . . . backwards! And I want you to come . . . to fill me. I want you to fill me!'

'Certainly, Mrs Dexter.'

All change.

Down she went, her cheek buried in a pillow, bum in the air. I got up behind her and fed in Brutus, slick as a hot knife through butter, making her cry out with delight.

'Oh, Randy . . . Randy . . . go . . . *go*!'

I went.

By heck, she really lapped it up. She bellowed and yelled, thumped the pillow and clawed the sheets and hit one final, glorious climax as I exploded both barrels into her.

'WwwwwOOOOOOWWW!' I roared.

'OHHHHHHHHHH!' she thundered. 'Ohhh . . . Randy . . . Randy . . .'

'Ohhh . . . Mrs Dexter . . . Mrs Dexter . . .'

'That's *hot* . . . scalding! . . . wonderful . . .!'

'It *certainly* was.'

It took us three or four minutes to subside, extricate, and collapse in each other's arms.

'You *naughty* boy . . .' she murmured exhaustedly. 'Where *did* you get all that from?'

'My piggy bank . . . I've been saving up.'

'For years, by the feel of things,' she chuckled and snuggled into me. 'Do you feel sleepy?'

'Mmm . . . so-so. How about you?'

'So-so. I feel incredibly relaxed . . . all floaty and weightless . . . and I think my legs have dropped off.' She gave a wicked little laugh. 'In short, superbly screwed.'

'So do I,' I laughed. 'You really go a bit.'

'*I* go a bit! My dear boy, you ought to be on the *receiving* end of that thing. I'm not too sure it doesn't constitute actual bodily harm. But *very* lovely.'

'Enjoyed it, hm?'

'I feel ten years younger. Thank you, Randy . . .'

'Thank *you*, Mrs Dexter.'

'Miraculous.' She breathed a deeply satisfied sigh and wriggled into me, lapsed into contemplative silence . . . and in minutes we were both fast asleep.

When I woke she was sitting up in bed in a housecoat, smoking a cigarette and sipping coffee.

'Hello,' I said. 'How long have you been awake? What time is it?'

'Ten o'clock. I've only just woken and made some coffee. I was worried about you getting home . . . *and* getting out of the gate this time of night. The gate poses a bit of a problem, doesn't it?'

'No. I can cut round the back and slip over the wall. No problem.'

'You're so beautifully confident, Randy, I adore it. But you *will* have to go home?'

I shrugged. 'Not necessarily, Mrs Dexter. No one will know if I sleep there or not.'

She relaxed visibly, smiled with relief. 'That's wonderful. I was hoping you'd stay a little longer. I don't think I could bear sleeping in this big bed without you tonight.'

'You'd like me to stay all night?' I asked, surprised.

'Would you?'

'Well, yes, certainly, if that's what you want, and if it's all right with you. I mean, nobody's likely to call or anything?'

'No, nobody's likely to call. Thank you, Randy . . . you're so understanding. Are you hungry?'

I thought about it. 'Mm, getting peckish.'

'Then I shall make us something.' Her eyes went to the bottom of the bed. 'Try that on, see how it fits.'

It was a dressing gown in pale yellow silk, edged in brown. I got off the bed, knowing her eyes were on me, and slipped it on.

'It's perfect!'

'It's yours.'

'Oh, Mrs Dexter . . .'

'So little, Randy, for so very much. My dear, it delights me to see you nicely dressed and to see your appreciation of lovely things. I will find more for you.'

'I don't know what to say . . .'

'Say nothing, your expression is thanks enough. Come . . .' she got off the bed and came round it. 'How would you like a nice deep, hot bath and then something to eat?'

'Sounds terrific.'

'Right – well, you go and draw the bath and I shall start something in the kitchen. Put lots of nice smelly oil in, we'll pamper ourselves.'

We parted company – rejoining in ten minutes, by which time I was waist-deep in suds.

'Come on in, the water's lovely!'

She stood on the edge of the bath, untied her sash and dropped the gown to the floor, then came down the steps into the water, launching out towards me doing the breast stroke. She reached for my extended hand and stood up, coming hard against me and gasping with surprise. 'Randy . . . !' With an appalled laugh her hand went underwater to feel what she'd run into. 'Comfort . . . you randy devil. What brought this on?'

'You, standing up there naked . . . standing here naked . . . and doing that.'

'My God, what a libido. I'd have thought you'd had enough for one night.'

'Have *you*?'

'I thought I had, but . . . you've just changed my mind.'

Slickly she slipped him between her legs and clasped me tightly round the waist. 'This is *awful*!' she giggled. 'It's as bad as being on one's honeymoon . . . or better. Are you always this sexy?'

'No,' I lied. 'It's you.'

'We'll make ourselves ill,' she laughed. 'Hey, how would you like to wash me?'

'You *know* how I'd like to wash you.'

She extricated herself, went to collect soap and a sponge from the side of the bath and brought them to me.

'Turn round,' I said.

I covered her flawless back with soap and sponged her down. 'Is that nice?'

'Wonderful,' she sighed. 'You're so gentle.'

'Now your front.'

She turned, finger poised. 'No games, now.'

'Certainly not,' I said, throwing the sponge away.

I soaped her breasts and took them in my hands, squeezed them gently, drawing out the nipples between finger and thumb. She buckled at the knees.

'Oh, Randy, don't . . .' she pleaded woefully. 'You know what will happen.'

I didn't answer, just kept right on doing it.

A minute of this and she was on her way. Releasing one breast I dropped my hand underwater and found her, caressed her. She fell hard against me, jerked into me, with me, coming on with a tremendous rush and an explosive shout that echoed shatteringly around the bathroom.

'DAAAAAAHHHHHHH!'

She collapsed, clung to me, jerking herself to conclusion with plaintive little gasps and bewildered mews. 'Randy, you devil . . . Oh, that was lovely. Ohhh . . .'

'What's the matter?'

'I want *you*, that's what's the matter.'

'How? Where?'

'Here . . . !'

Grasping my hand, she pulled me urgently to the side of the bath, then draped herself over it, her back to me, spreading wide to receive me. In I went, hard as iron, slipping my hands to her waist for maximum leaverage.

This one was a corker, fast and furious, mutually desired rape, a slam, bang thrash that more than made up in intensity what it lacked in duration and finesse.

Pow!

We were there in a wild photo-finish, filling the room with jubilant bellows, collapsing with laughter at the speed and greed of it, the sheer excitement of driving, animal copulation.

'Wheeeeeee!' she cheered.

'Wooooowww!' I gasped, falling against her and hugging her.

'Oh, Randy, randy . . . what *am* I going to do with you?'

'More of what you've just done. I can take an awful lot of this.'

'My God, what *have* I let myself in for?'

'The time of your life, Mrs Dexter.'

'I'm having it . . . I'm having it!'

We bathed leisurely, floated languidly, just pottered about and laughed at each other.

'What a wonderful thing it is, joyous fornication,' she observed with a wistful sigh. 'I feel so young at heart. I never dreamed I would feel this way again. You've brought me incredibly alive. By the time most women reach forty, all this has gone from their lives – if it was ever a part of them. You've made me believe that forty is hardly any age at all.'

'It isn't, not for a woman like you, Mrs Dexter.'

'Oh, I was beginning to feel it, Randy. I was feeling spent, useless . . . and that this sort of fun was gone forever.'

I thought about Billy Chang and reasoned that either she was fibbing or he was a very poor operator, prefering, of course, to believe the latter. Nah, I just couldn't see her having the same sort of fun with him. He'd be strictly wham, bam, thank you, ma'm, a quick ten minutes and out.

'Well . . .' she smiled. '*Now* are you feeling hungry?'

'Starved.'

'I should jolly-well think so. Come on, let's eat. I'm doing you soup, omelet and fruit, how does that sound?'

'Like a banquet.'

An hour later we were back in bed, this time really *in* it. She'd set the alarm for eight, giving me time to skip over the wall and come through the main gate as though I was reporting for work as usual.

'Tired, now?' she smiled, reaching for the light switch.

'Mm . . . so-so. That was a pretty good sleep we had before.'

'Sleep,' she commanded. 'You have a day's work to do tomorrow. I can sleep late, but you can't.'

'No, ma'm.'

She turned out the light and curled into me in the semi-darkness, a sliver of light coming in from the hall to take the agony out of total blackness.

'Randy . . .'

'Yes, Mrs Dexter?'

'Do you really like me?'

'Of course, Mrs Dexter. I wouldn't be here if I didn't.'

'No, you wouldn't, would you. I like you . . . very much. I can't thank you enough for tonight.'

'Well, I'll say again, it was entirely my pleasure.'

She gave a chuckle. 'You certainly *seemed* to be enjoying yourself. How long do you suppose you could keep this output up?'

I shrugged. 'Depends on the amount of encouragement I got . . . thirty . . . forty years, I suppose.'

She laughed throatily and snuggled close.

'Goodnight, Randy . . .'

'Goodnight, Mrs Dexter.'

I suppose we slept about four hours then surfaced simultaneously, turned over by mutual consent, so that now I cuddled her and instantly became aware of her simmering nakedness, close-fitted into my belly.

I slipped my arm through hers and found her breast. She murmured softly and wriggled into me, bringing me wide awake and beginning to grow.

Unspeaking, she opened her thighs and let me through, groaning as The Brute made contact with her erogenous vulva, then, urgently, she was turning onto her back and pulling me over her, her legs spread wide, her hand guiding me deeply, deeply in.

'Oh, Randy . . .' she gasped. 'Please fuck me . . . *fuck* me!'

And, for the third time of asking, the boy selflessly complied.

CHAPTER EIGHT

As I stood by the door she came to me, kissed me on the cheek and simultaneously stuffed something into the breast pocket of my shirt (which she had ironed while I was eating a boiled egg breakfast).

'What's this?' I frowned, all innocence.

'A small present, to keep the wolf at bay.'

'Oh, Mrs Dexter . . .'

'Sssshh! I insist.'

'But . . .' I held up the carrier bag containing the shirts and dressing gown, '. . . you've already . . .'

'Those are nothing. Be good, now, or I won't ring again for service. Go, now, or you'll be late . . . and mind how you climb that wall, we don't want you losing anything in the process, do we?'

I grinned at her. 'No, ma'm, I'll be very careful.'

She opened the door and popped her head out. 'All clear . . .'

I slipped through, whispering, 'Bye . . . and thanks ever so much.'

She replied with a blown kiss and quickly closed the door.

On my toes I crept down the hall, exited through the rear door, made straight for the garages out back, slipped behind them, climbed an eight-foot wall with the aid of a dustbin and dropped into the road.

Ten minutes later I was strolling nonchalantly up to the main gate.

'Morning, Dan.'

' 'Ello, mate, you look very chipper this morning.' His eyes went to the carrier bag. 'Bin doing some shopping?'

'Yes, bought a couple of shirts on the way to work.'

'How are things going, all right?'

'Couldn't be better. How's the list coming along?'

'I'll have it finished by tonight. Pick it up on your way out.'

'Thanks, I will . . . ooh, no I can't. I'm doing a bit of overtime tonight . . . probably won't be finished by the time you leave.'

'Oh, aye,' he grinned. 'Doin' some last night, too, weren't you? I was waiting for you to come out.'

'Er, yes . . . yes, Mrs Dexter in Three had a spot of trouble with her sink drain. Had to clear it out after hours.'

'Oh, yeah? What time did you finish? Must've bin after seven, 'cos I don't leave till seven.'

'Yes, it must have been just after that. Tough job.'

'Her husband's away, isn't he.' He gave me a man-to-man leer. 'Anything happen?'

I frowned, puzzled. 'Happen? Like what?'

'Come orf it, you know what I mean. Did she make any "unseemly advances" to you.'

'Good God, no. No, she gave me a cuppa tea . . . and we chatted while I was working, but that's all. Hey, you're ribbing me. Nothing like that would happen here.'

'Really?' he grinned. 'Well, we'll see. Who're you doing overtime for tonight?'

'Oh, er, Miss Roget in Forty Eight.'

'The artist bird, eh? What're you doin' for her, posin' in the nude?'

'Nah, don't be daft,' I laughed. 'No, she's got a couple of jobs she wants doing up there but she's working during the day and can't have me banging about. Asked me to do them after hours.'

'One of these days you're going to find yourself bein' raped by one of these birds, you mark my words. You'll be crawlin' in here on your hands and knees.'

'Chance'd be a fine thing,' I laughed. 'Well, I'd better get on, Dan. I'll collect that list tomorrow morning.'

'Happy posing!' he chortled.

I walked on. Out of his view I took whatever Mrs Dexter

had given me out of my pocket . . . and damn near died. It was two tenners . . . twenty quid!

Blimey O'Reilly, twenty quid for doing what came not only naturally, but, with her, delightfully. At this rate I'd be telling the owners to stuff their room in a few months. I'd be able to afford my own flat, or buy the bleeding building!

Jack Berryweed was there and in jovial mood.

'Mornin', Randy. How'd you get on at Mrs Dexter's last night?'

'Fixed her up a treat, Mr Berryweed.'

'Good lad. I appreciate you doing that.'

'She did, too,' I said. 'Oh, yes, I've got a bit more overtime tonight, Miss Roget in Forty Eight. She's got a couple of carpentry jobs she wants doing, but says she can't stand me banging about during the day while she's working. Is it all right with you?'

'With me? Of course it's all right. What you do after five is your own business, and if happens to please the residents, I'm more than happy.' He regarded me over his glasses. 'Reckon there's a bob or two in it for you? It ought to be worth something to her if you're working overtime.'

I shrugged, nobly. 'Aw, I don't mind, Mr Berryweed. As I said, I don't do much at night, and I'd just as soon be helping somebody as sitting watching tellie or in the boozer.'

He shook his head. 'You're a rare lad, Randy. But don't worry, you'll get paid back. As I told you, these folk can be very generous to people they like, and the way you're goin', I reckon you're goin' to be the darling of the Mansions!'

'Nah,' I grinned, abashed. 'I'm not doing it for that, Mr Berryweed. It's just . . . well, as the old song says, "If I can help somebody as I go along, then my living has not been in vain". Sounds corny, I know, but it's the way I feel.'

'Quite right, too,' he sniffed, and I swear there were tears in his eyes. 'Well, now, got a couple of jobs for you . . .'

The day dragged by with agonizing slowness, and all I

could think of during it was getting up to Rachel Roget's at five.

What *would* transpire? I asked myself.

She'd probably play it cool at first, even pretend she was painting me! But as the evening wore on . . .

My imagination took off, the vision culminating in a glorious French thrash in her bedroom, paints abandoned, pretense abandoned, everything abandoned. She looked the type, a real tiger.

I couldn't wait for five o'clock.

At last it came.

'Well, I'll be off up to Forty Eight, Mr Berryweed.'

'Yes, all right, lad. See you tomorra, then. Don't work too hard, now, we don't want you exhausted.'

'No, I'll watch it. Goodnight, Mr Berryweed.'

I almost ran over to the East Wing and leapt up the stairs rather than wait for a lift.

Approaching Forty Eight, I slowed, and rang the bell, wishing my heart wouldn't thud so hard.

The door opened.

It was the maid, though I didn't recognize her for a second – she was dressed in civvies, a coat on over a frock.

'Ah, m'sieur, please to come in.' I stepped past her. 'Pliz, go through to the studio, it's next to ze bedroom where you feexed ze curtains. Mademoiselle Roget is waiting for you.'

'Oh,' I gulped. 'Are you . . . going out?'

'Oui, m'sieur. Bon soir . . . good night.'

'Erm, yes . . .'

Out she went, closing the door.

Blimey . . . so *that's* the way she was playing it, straight from the shoulder, no messing about. Well, well, well . . .

Girding my loins, I went down the hall, crossed the lounge and entered the corridor, announcing my presence with a loud cough and a call. 'Miss Roget . . . ?'

'Come through, Mister Comfort . . .'

Lovely voice . . . pure seduction.

The door to the studio was open. She was working behind a big canvas on an easel, her back to the window. I glanced quickly around the room. It was bare, spartan, the minimum of furniture and, surprisingly, one of those gymnasium exercise bicycles set on a raised wooden plinth.

She came from behind the canvas and took my breath away. Again she was wearing jeans and blouse but this time the blouse was almost transparent, thin as thin, and through it I could plainly see her breasts. Ho ho, these French birds . . . they just don't care!

'Hello,' she smiled, wiping a droop of dark hair from her face. 'You're very punctual.'

'Couldn't wait to begin,' I grinned. 'How're the curtains, still up?'

'But of course. I'm sure anything *you* put up, stays up.'

Oh, you naughty madam. Did you ever hear anything so blatantly suggestive? I suddenly revised my fantasy, the way things were going, she wouldn't even *pretend* to paint.

'Beats me how they, hm, fell down in the first place,' I smiled slyly, letting her know I was on to her little game.

'I believe I do,' she answered soberly. 'The apartment was re-painted a week ago. The painter took down the rail to paint behind it, and I can only suppose his idiot assistant, a very young boy, merely pushed the screws in with his fingers when he reinstated it. He certainly looked capable.'

'Oh,' I said, flattened by her obviously sincere tone. 'Well, yes . . . that . . . would be an explanation.'

'Are you ready to begin?' she smiled, not at all flirtatiously. 'We must catch as much of the daylight as possible.'

'Oh, yes . . . certainly. What would you like me to do?'

Her eyes went past me to the mounted exercise bike. 'I would like you to ride that.'

'Hm?' I turned, perplexed. 'Ride that?'

'You don't mind?'

'Oh, no . . . no, certainly not.'

'And I would like you to change into a pair of cycling shorts and a vest. I have them in the bedroom. Would you come through?'

So . . . all was not lost!

I followed her into the bedroom, next door. There on her bed were the shorts, vest and a pair of cycling shoes.

'There,' she said. 'Please come through when you've changed.'

And then she was gone, closing the door.

Hm, I thought. Well, all was still not lost.

I changed quickly, feeling a right narna in the gear, then returned to the studio.

'Good,' she smiled. 'You certainly look the part. Now, if you'd just get on the bicycle . . .'

I climbed on.

'Would you pedal for me, please?'

I'd never been on one of these things before and got the shock of my life when I tried to pedal. There was some form of resistance, a pressure against the wheel, making it very hard going, like cycling through heavy mud.

'Wow!' I laughed.

'Keep going, please, I want to gauge your reaction precisely.'

'Oh. Er, mind if I ask what you're painting?'

She grinned, devilishly. 'Agony . . . the torture of the professional athlete when pushed to the limit of his endurance.'

I gulped.

'Keep going,' she said, turning her attention to the pressure adjuster between the handlebars and giving it a turn – for the worse.

'Oh, boy . . .' I said. 'That's rough.'

'Good . . . that is what I want, that expression of strain. Keep pedalling like that, it is perfect.'

Urgently, she strode back to the easel and disappeared behind the canvas, picked up her pallet and began. A moment later her head popped out. 'Keep pedalling!'

I pedalled.

A minute later the strain began . . . two minutes and sweat was pouring down my face . . . three and I was panting like an old dog . . .

'Keep going, that's wonderful!' she enthused, painting like the clappers.

'God, this is torture, miss . . .'

'Precisely! Your expression is perfect! It is the face of a professional athlete nearing the end of a killing hundred-mile race . . . now, harder . . . pedal harder!'

Oh, fucking hell . . . my legs were dropping off . . . my thigh muscles were screaming . . . calves bulging like coconuts . . . sweat was cascading down my throbbing face. Lips bared and teeth clenched I struggled on and on, every turn of the pedal excruciating hell. I tried thinking of other things to deaden the pain, thoughts of all the lovely money I was earning. Two pounds an hour . . . two pounds an *hour*! I'd be lucky to last fifteen minutes!

'Oh, miss . . .' I gasped, fucked, finished. 'I can't go on . . .'

'You must, you must! The finish line is in sight! The crowd's are cheering . . . you are winning! But the next man is only yards behind you . . . and he's coming up fast! He's putting in a final spurt! Go . . . go . . . faster . . . faster!'

'Ohh . . . ohhh . . . oh, my legs . . .'

'Faster . . . faster!'

'I can't . . . I can't!'

'You must . . . you will . . . you *can*!'

'I'm dyin' . . . dyin' . . .'

'Die over the line! This is your great, final achievement . . . you *must* win! This is the pinnacle of your long professional career! If you lose this race, you have lost everything you've ever worked . . . striven . . . tortured yourself for! Throw *everything* you've got into one last, tremendous burst! And go . . . go! . . . GO!'

I fell off the bike, then . . . lay groaning with terrible

agony, my leg muscles bunched up with diabolical cramp like tangled knitting wool. 'Oh . . . ! ahhh . . . ! eeehh!'

She didn't take a blind bit of notice. She was still painting like fury, popping out every now and then to take a peek at my face, then darting back for another dab.

'Oh, me legs . . . me legs!'

'Excellent . . . *excellent! Just* what I wanted!'

I got to my knees, grabbed the bike and hauled myself up, and fell straight down again. Believe me, I've had some knee-tremblers in my time, but this was ludicrous. They were shaking like coal sifters! Weak? They were wobbly columns of sponge rubber!

'Oh, miss, me legs . . . I can't do any more . . . I can't go on!'

'Fine,' she muttered. 'Well, you can get changed . . .'

She didn't give a stuff!

I tried standing again but fell down again and finally exited on my hands and knees.

It took me ten minutes to get dressed and by then, if anything, my legs were worse. I think gangrene had set in. They were so weak I had to edge my way into the studio along the wall, grabbing doors and things to stay upright.

She was still at it, painting like there was no tonight, never mind tomorrow.

'You all right?' she murmured.

'Ha!' I laughed. 'I think the bones have dropped out of my legs.'

'You were superb – just the reaction I wanted.'

'You mean . . . that's it? You don't want me any more?'

She popped her head out, grinning. 'You want to do some more?'

'No! I mean . . . I couldn't . . .'

'I know. You lasted very well . . . I didn't expect more than ten minutes.'

I gaped at her. 'You didn't? But you mentioned three hours work . . . dinner.'

She popped out again smiling archly. 'A little subterfuge, I'm afraid. If you had known what you were in for, would you have volunteered?'

I coughed. 'Well . . .'

'Of course, you wouldn't. But don't worry, I shall make it worth your while.'

She laid down the pallet and came out, wiping her hands on a cloth. 'Come . . .'

'Er . . . may I see what you've painted?'

She shrugged. 'Certainly. I did most of it before you arrived. I had only the face to fill in.'

I went round the easel. The painting was marvellous. It was me . . . approaching the finishing line of a big race, my face contorted, muscles straining, on the very edge of complete collapse.

'A remarkable likeness,' I said. 'That's exactly how I felt . . . feel.'

'Never mind, your legs will be back to normal tomorrow. A little stiff, perhaps, but you'll be all right. Come with me now . . .'

In the lounge she opened a handbag and handed me some money. 'There's a little extra there to compensate for dinner. Take your girlfriend to a nice restaurant instead. And thank you very much, you were very helpful.'

I put on a brave face until she'd closed the door after me, then I gave vent to the pains that were shooting up my legs.

This may sound ridiculous, but it took me a good 15 minutes to reach the main gate. Dan Brogan saw me coming and stood there scratching his head.

'What the 'oly 'ell's up with you?' he laughed. 'Got corns or somethin'? You look like you're walking on eggs.'

'It's me legs, Dan. I was doing a . . . a crouching-down job for Miss Roget and got cramp. They don't half hurt.'

'A crouching-down job, hey?' he sniffed. 'Kinky. Here, I've got that list for you.'

He popped into his hut and handed me a sheet of paper.

'Thanks a lot, Dan, I appreciate it. Here . . . have a drink on me.'

'Ah, no, mate, that's all right . . .'

I pulled out the loot Rachel Roget had given me and opened it. Ten quid! A fiver and five ones. The sight of it somehow eased the ache in my legs. I handed two singles to Dan who stopped pretending and took them.

'Thanks, Randy, I shall drink your health soon as I'm finished. Mind how you go now . . . blimey, you are in trouble.'

Walking stiff-legged, like my boots were filled with broken glass, I trundled out of the gate and made my way home, climbed the stairs to my room and didn't have the nerve to face the ordeal again, so I stayed in and missed dinner altogether.

What a turn-up. Not too much like my fantasy. Still, there was little Fran to look forward to tomorrow, and an early night tonight was just what I needed.

Ah yes, I could picture it. A knock on her door, she'd open it, welcome me in, and bob's your uncle. I'd make it late in the afternoon so I could spend a good hour with her.

Wednesday, I just knew, was going to be one exceedingly beautiful day.

How wrong can a guy get!

CHAPTER NINE

It started off all right, nice sunny day, not too much stiffness in the legs, and thoughts of Fran to cheer me, so much so that I arrived in Jack Berryweed's office in tip-top form.

'Here,' he said, 'had an urgent call from Twenty Six, Viscount Ballymore's place.'

'Oh, he's home?'

'No, he ain't. But he's got two young nieces of his staying here for a few days . . . and they've gorn and broken a pane of glass in the bathroom. You'll have to measure up and get a new piece cut at Loxley's, round the corner.'

'Right, I'll be off.'

Two nieces, hm, this sounded promising.

Twenty Six was just upstairs, second floor rear. I nipped up the stairs, feeling the old legs a bit, and rang the bell, picturing two ravishingly lovely blonde creatures in their early twenties . . . and was shockingly disappointed.

'Yes?'

The face in the doorway was not, to say the least, beautiful. To be honest it was downright plain, horsey. She was a blonde all right, just, but more mouse than golden corn, and her only redeeming feature, as far as I could see, was a reasonable body, clad in blue jeans and a yellow T-shirt with a big red apple on the front.

I devastated her with a smile. 'Good morning, miss . . . I'm the . . .'

'Oh, the bog window, come in.'

Charming. Top-drawer bird like her calling it a bog. By gum, you don't get much for a thousand quid a year at these posh private schools. Her old man must be doing his nut.

As I stepped into the hallway, another top-drawer voice,

with an edge on it like a bread knife, called through from the lounge. 'Who is it, Clarrie?'

'The maintenance wallah, come to fix the bog window!' yelled Clarrie.

'Oh, *su*-per!'

Out she came, Winnie the Witch, a jungle of dark, frizzy hair framing a comically ugly face. She was also in jeans and T-shirt, both wring-dyed in dazzling purple – a plump little thing with enormous knockers and thighs of steel. Must have been deadly on the hockey field, and not bad over the sticks, either.

Their ages? About nineteen, going on six. You could tell from the vocabulary.

'Good morning,' I bade her, not knowing whether to bow or not. How did you address a viscount's niece? 'Slut' seemed appropriate in this case.

'Ring-a-*ding*,' she replied enthusiastically, making an approving face at Clarrie. 'Are you resident or imported?' she asked me, these frrrightfully posh voices not matching the faces, somehow.

'Resident, miss . . . though I don't actually *live* here.'

'No . . . you wouldn't, would you.'

Snobby bitch.

'The er, window?' I suggested, wanting to get out of there before I was tempted to clout both of them.

'*She* broke it,' Winnie announced triumphantly, pointing at Clarrie who was lurking behind me.

I heard an appalled gasp. 'Anthea, you fucking little liar, *you* did it!'

'Didn't.'

'You did! She threw a jar of cold cream at me and I ducked.'

I turned, realising I was being addressed, my mind frozen by the unexpectedness of the foul language . . . and not altogether unexcited by it. What did we have here, then? A couple of trollops? I did a swift re-appraisal of them, cutting away the snobby dross, and discovered a couple of birds I still didn't *fancy* much, but who might be good for a dirty laugh or two.

'Oh, so that's what happened,' I commented.

'No, it bloody isn't,' answered Anthea. 'She's a congenital liar . . . makes up the most *appalling* fibs.'

Clarrie made a lunge for her and she fled, screaming, but stopped in the lounge doorway and pulled tongues at her sister. A right couple of idiots. 'I'll get you for that,' threatened Clarrie.

'Up yours, cousin *dear*.'

Oh, so they weren't sisters.

Clarrie turned to me. 'Come on, I'll show you the thing ...'

'I know where the bathroom is, thanks.'

'So, suit yourself.'

She turned and made a dive for Anthea and they disappeared into the lounge, squealing like stuck pigs.

The bathroom was in a right old mess, clothes, towels, make-up, tissues strewn all over the place. I shifted half-a-hundredweight of underclothes off the toilet lid to get at the window and discovered a magazine underneath. It was 'STUD', full of naked fellas with big dicks and muscles for brains. So that was their little turn-on! *Su*-per.

I opened the window inwards and while I was chipping away the broken glass, I could hear them giggling out in the hall, whispering to each other, and instinct told me the little buggers were hatching something. Make no mistake about it, two daft birds together are worse than any two lads for mischief, and I wouldn't put anything past these two. So it came as no surprise when the dark one, Anthea, sidled into the bathroom, innocent as you please, and sat on the edge of the bath to watch me work.

Clarrie, I sensed, was out in the hall, right behind me, and through the corner of my eye I could feel Anthea memoing little signals to her.

'Been doing this job long?' Anthea enquired nonchalantly.

'Here? – since last Friday, miss.'

'Oh, you are new. Like it here?'

'Yes, very nice, miss, thank you.'

'What time do you finish at night?'

'Five o'clock, miss . . . Monday to Friday.'

'And then what do you do?'

'I go home.'

'Yes, but to where?'

'Oh, not far. I have a roo . . . an apartment close by.'

'How cozy. Are you married?'

'No, miss.'

'Engaged?'

'No, miss.'

'Girl friend?'

'Six or seven, miss,' I grinned.

'Yes, I'll bet.'

'Oh, why, miss?'

'You look the type.'

'And what type's that, miss?'

'Sexy.'

I gave a cough. Ber-*rum*-te-dum-de-dum . . . I continued to chip away the glass as though I hadn't heard.

'You didn't bring any new glass,' she said.

'No, I've got to measure up and get it cut.'

'That means you'll have to come back.'

'Yes, miss.'

'When will that be?'

'I hope later on this afternoon. I'll phone the order through now and they'll deliver it, then I'll put it in.'

She turned to address Clarrie. 'He says he'll put it in later this afternoon.'

'*Su*-per,' giggled Clarrie.

Little monkeys, they were trying to get me going!

'How long will it take you to put it in?' enquired Anthea, stifling her laughter, though not very successfully.

Fine, if this is the game they wanted to play . . . 'Oh, not long, miss, I'm pretty quick at getting it in.'

'He says not long, he's pretty quick at getting it in,' she relayed to Clarrie.

'Super *du*-per!'

'I'm sure you're very good with your hands,' remarked Anthea. 'Very expert. What's your name?'

'Randy Comfort,' I said distinctly and she almost fell in the bath laughing.

'I missed that!' complained Clarrie.

'His name . . .' chortled Anthea, spelling it out to her, 'is . . . Randy . . . Comfort!'

'Ah, he's putting you on . . .'

I turned. 'No, really, that's my name, Randolph Comfort. Randy for short.'

'*Price*less!' hooted Clarrie and now they were both doubled up. 'I vote that . . . the Name of the Year!'

They split their sides for a few more minutes, then Anthea, wiping tears from her cheeks, gasped, 'It must lead to some very embarrassing moments for you . . . imagine a girl coming up to you and asking, "Are you Randy?"'

I turned to her, shrugging. 'I'd tell her yes. That wouldn't be embarrassing, it'd be the truth.'

'Oh ho,' she laughed, throwing a glance at Clarrie. '*Are* you randy, Randy?'

I didn't answer. 'There, that's got it – now I just have to measure it.'

'Ohhh!' she whooped. 'Clarrie, he's going to measure it!'

'This I *must* see!'

She crowded in, peering round me as I flourished my ruler.

'Oh, he means the rotten old window,' groaned Anthea.

'Sixteen inches . . . by nine and a half . . .' I muttered.

'Ooh, what a whopper,' breathed Anthea.

'There you are, ladies, all done. I'll be back later to fit it in.'

'We'll be waiting,' Anthea said coyly. 'Don't let us down, now.'

'As if I'd do a thing like that. Goodbye.'

They both saw me to the door.

'See you later!' I waved, and they closed the door.

Phew! Right couple of tear-aways, those two. No doubt they'd have something amusing lined up for me when I went back, like a bucket of whitewash over the door, filled with pig-iron.

I returned to the office, phoned in the measurements and the shop promised delivery by three o'clock. Fine, I could nip up and put the glass in and make Fran my excuse for leaving, otherwise they'd keep me nattering all afternoon. A joke was a joke but anything more than ten minutes with those two would tend to get pretty yawny.

However, these arrangements were not to be. Three o'clock came but no glass came with it. Three thirty arrived . . . four o'clock. Forget the glass, son, it's time for Fran!

'Mister Berryweed, I'll have to leave that glass job and see to Miss Drew's bathroom cabinet. I promised to go back this afternoon.'

'Yers . . .' he said doubtfully. 'But you can't leave them two ladies without glass in the toilet.'

I shrugged. 'I'll have to do it later. Would you get on to the shop and find out what's happened? I'll be back before five.'

'Yes, all right . . .'

With fast beating heart I scarpered over to the East Wing, cursing fate that I'd now have to cut Fran a bit short. Still, an awful lot can be accomplished in half an hour if the parties concerned properly apply themselves.

Whistling silently, I hot-footed it along the corridor and stopped outside Forty, tidied myself up and rang the bell – then nipped away from the door and flattened myself against the wall.

Footsteps approached. I could see her in my mind's eye,

all neat and cuddly in her little maid's uniform, impatient to see me.

The door opened.

I sprang out. '*He*-llo, my darl . . .'

Oh, Jesus . . . it was Suzie Drew! . . . tall, svelte, blonde, and blistering with anger. She speared me with smouldering green eyes, raked me from head to toe, frowning furiously, then spat, 'Who the hell are *you*!'

'Er . . . I . . .oh, God . . . I'm terribly sorry, Miss Drew, I . . . oh . . .!'

'Well, who . . .'

'Randolph Comfort, miss . . . I've come to put up your cathroom bab . . . your bathroom cabinet.'

'Really.' She pinned me to the wall with a glower of inate suspicion. 'Well, you'd better come in and do it, quickly.'

'Yes, miss . . . certainly, miss.'

I entered, followed her perfumed wake into the lounge where she peeled away and snatched up the telephone, snapping at me. 'You know where it is . . . and I want you out of here in ten minutes!'

'Yes, miss . . .'

Now what had gone wrong! She was supposed to be out all day. Oh, bloody hell, what a let-down. There I was, mentally all horned-up for Frannie, and didn't doubt she was equally ready, and now this. I should've known it was all too good to be true.

I reached the bathroom without seeing a sign of Fran. Was she still here? Had she been fired?

I got the cabinet on the wall, levelled it off, and was marking the holes when Suzie Drew began her telephone tirade. By God, she was really blistering somebody . . . calling them all the incompetant, unprofessional berks it had ever been her misfortune to encounter.

Then, into this barrage of invective, came a 'Pssssst!' from the doorway.

It was Fran!

I dropped the cabinet and went over to her, pulling a face at the racket Suzie was making.

'Hello, love . . . what happened!'

'She didn't go!' she whispered.

'Obviously.'

'At least she went to the airport but came straight back. The session had been cancelled at the last minute, but somebody had forgotten to ring her.'

'Oh, cripes . . .'

'She's livid!'

'You do surprise me. And *I* made things worse, I hid round the corner and jumped out at her and said "*He*-llo, my darling", thinking it was you!'

Her hand flew to her mouth. 'No! Oh, gawd . . .'

'Listen, I'd better get this thing up in a hurry, she's given me ten minutes. You'll have to give me a call about something else – kick a hole in the wall – when she's safely out of the way.'

'Right!'

The telephone slammed down. 'Frances!'

'Coming, Miss Drew . . .!'

She blew me a kiss and scarpered.

I got the cabinet up in double-quick time and when I went back into the lounge they'd both disappeared. Never having been a bloke to purposely court disaster, I wasn't about to start now, so I crept across the deep pile carpet and silently let myself out, breathing a sigh of relief.

Well, there went a beautiful dream.

I returned to the office feeling distinctly jaded, and in no mood to face the two idiots in Twenty Six.

'That was quick,' remarked Berryweed. 'Your glass has come, the van had a puncture. What's the time now . . . four twenty. Oh, well, you'll just have time to do that, then.'

'Yes, Mister Berryweed.'

'Something the matter, son? You look a bit piqued.'

'No, no . . . just a bit tired, I expect. I'll have an early night tonight.'

'Yes, I would, and no more overtime for a bit. You're overdoing it perhaps.'

Huh, chance'd be a fine thing.

I collected the glass and putty and took the lift upstairs, rang the bell of Twenty Six. Clarrie answered the door, changed from jeans and top into a blue floral housecoat and looking as though she'd washed her hair.

'He's here, Anthea!' she sang out.

'*Su*-per!'

I stepped inside, coming face-to-face with Anthea who was also attired in a housecoat – red satin with lots of frills – and also looked as though *she'd* washed *her* hair. In fact, dressed like this, they weren't a bad-looking pair of birds, though not first-choicers, if you know what I mean. Perhaps not even seconds, but nevertheless they had something.

'You kept your promise,' she observed.

'Well, I couldn't leave you without a window in the bathroom, now, could I? You might catch your deaths.'

'Highly unlikely,' remarked Clarrie, dryly, 'considering we've bathed in sub-zero temperatures at school for the past umpteen years. Anyway, you're a bit late, we've just had baths and washed our hairs.'

Anthea giggled. 'Yes, our hairs.'

And away we go again!

'May we come and watch you?' enquired Anthea, bright-eyed with mischief.

'Yes, of course.'

'Would you like a drink while you're performing?'

I grinned. 'Well, yes, thank you . . . if you're having one.'

'We've already had one, but we're going to have another. Uncle will have a fit when he checks his scotch, but who cares? We're on holiday and we are going to do precisely what we like, aren't we, Clarrie?'

'Pre-cisely,' nodded Clarrie.

'Just . . . broken up, then, have you, for the summer?' I asked.

They both giggled.

'We don't acutally call it "breaking up",' dear Clarrie explained loftily, 'but you've got the right idea.'

'Where do you go to school?'

'Scotland,' answered Anthea. 'As bloody far north as you can get without falling in the rotten sea. Go through, you two, I'll get the drinkies.'

Clarrie and I went through.

Anthea followed in moments, carrying in a little gilt tray with three crystal glasses of what looked like scotch and water.

'How very jolly . . . a bathroom party. Here you are, darling . . . and Mister Randy . . .'

'Thank you.'

I took a glass.

'I shall propose the toast,' announced, Anthea, raising her glass. 'To . . . SIN!'

'To SIN!' responded Clarrie.

'Any reason in particular?' I asked.

'Yes,' said Anthea. 'Because we're fed up to the bloody back teeth BEING GOOD!'

'Here here,' said Clarrie. 'We have just suffered eleven excruciating years of boarding school . . . of being prim and proper and beautifully behaved English upper-class ladies and we now wish to taste the pleasures of EVIL!'

'EVIL!' cried Anthea, and took a hefty swig of her drink.

Clarrie followed suit.

I took a belt and coughed. It was *not* scotch and water, just scotch.

'Too strong for you, my mere man?' taunted Anthea.

I sniffed. 'Not at all, it's absolutely right. So, you've just left school, have you . . . congratulations. And what are you both going to do now?'

'For three months, nothing!' declaimed Clarrie. 'Day after

tomorrow we embark on a ring-a-ding tour of Europe and do not intend to go to bed before three in the morning one single night, at least to sleep! We intend to dance our bloody feet off in every disco between Le Havre and Rome, get smashed to our pretty eyeballs whenever the opportunity presents itself, and get laid every inch of the way! Hooray!'

'Olé!' cheered Anthea.

'Yoiks!'

'Tally-ho!'

'Sounds wonderful,' I said, turning my attention to the window before the scotch hit me. 'Wish I was coming with you.'

'Do!' exclaimed Anthea. 'You'd be terrif!'

'No, he wouldn't,' said Clarrie snootily. 'He's too prudish.'

I laughed. 'Me?!'

'Yes, you. You look distinctly virginal to me.'

I looked behind me, frowning. 'You must be thinking of another fellow.'

'I am not. You don't look to me as though you enjoy . . . games.'

Hey ho . . .

'Do *you* think he enjoys games, Anthea?'

'I don't know . . . it's possible.'

The old ticker was beginning to thump a bit, and the mouth had gone dry. 'What sort of games?' I enquired nonchalantly, taking, needing, another swig of scotch.

They giggled, having a lovely time.

I continued working on the window, my hands shaking a bit.

'We can't tell you . . . we'd have to show you,' answered Clarrie. 'We will, if you want, won't we, Anthea.'

'Oh, yes, we'll show you . . . if you want.'

I cleared my throat. 'Aherm . . . er, when?'

I caught their exchanged glances, their obvious delight.

'As soon as you've finished doing that,' Anthea answered flatly. 'When do you have to leave?'

I shrugged. 'No particular time.'

'*Shall* we show him, Clarrie?'

'Let's think about it while he's doing that.'

'You'll have to hurry up,' I said, 'it's nearly finished.'

'All right, we'll show you,' nodded Clarrie. 'Come through into the lounge when you're finished.'

And then, with a swish of housecoats, they were gone.

I puttied up, smiling to myself, wondering what they had in mind and how far they'd go. Not very, I thought. Their sort of bird was always ninety percent talk. It was the quiet ones like Fran that came across.

Ah, well, anything for a giggle.

I finished off and closed the window, had a wash, took another good gulp of scotch and floated through into the lounge, feeling no pain at all by now.

The lounge was in darkness, the heavy drapes drawn, and there was no sign of the girls. So, hide and seek was it. Grinning, I slipped off my shoes and tip-toed across the room, smashed into a side-table and cursed, producing a fit of giggling from a room down the hall.

Stealthily I tracked the source of sound, finding door after door wide open, each room in darkness.

The silly birds were going to jump out any minute and frighten the life out of me, so, prepared for it, I ventured into the first room.

What I wasn't prepared for was the pillow case that came whistling down over my head and shoulders, smothering me and binding my arms to my sides, and the piece of rope that simultaneously went round my ankles.

'Hey . . .!'

Something struck me in the back of the knees, buckling them, and down I went into the carpet.

'Hey, I'm suffocating!'

'Then stop struggling! Get his feet, Anthea!'

I was lifted bodily, carried across the room and dumped face-up on a bed. In a wink, rope went around both wrists and my arms were jerked out and up and secured to the bed head. 'Hey, *girls* . . .!'

'Shut up!' rapped Clarrie.

Now the rope that bound my ankles was pulled down and fastened to the bottom of the bed, and that nicely took care of Randolph Comfort.

'Girls, take this damned pillow-case off . . . please!'

Silence.

I lay still, listening. Not a sound.

I began to get panicky. Had they left me to sweat it out? Hell, I couldn't stand much of this.

'Girls . . . please! Come on, a joke's a joke but I'm suffocating! I'm all for fun but . . .'

Suddenly the pillow-case was lifted from my face – not removed, just raised. Fresh air streamed in. I breathed deeply. 'Wow . . .' But after a couple of breaths it was dropped again. 'Hey . . ! Ah, come on, girls . . . oooh!'

Somebody's hot hands were at the buckle of my belt. Two snicks and it was undone. The zipper was drawn down . . . then, in a giggling flurry of heaving and pulling my trousers shot down to my knees.

Instinctively I twisted, bucked, but only succeeded in helping them.

Now I really felt panicky . . . vulnerable. What were they going to do – paint my balls with shoe black? . . . or worse?

I tried to sit up but got nowhere.

'Lie still!' Anthea commanded. 'You'll only cut your hands off.'

'Ah, girls, no . . . come on . . .'

'Oh, we're coming,' threatened Clarrie.

Fingers sneaked into the top of my shorts. 'Waaaahh . . .!'

Down they came, joining my trousers.

There was another fit of giggling.

'Oooohhh . . .' said one.

'Gorgeous!' said the other.

Silence.

It was worse than the activity.

I lay there, tense with horrified anticipation, expecting anything from a pair of scissors to a red hot poker.

'Funny things, aren't they, Anthea?'

'But *su*-per . . .'

'Shall we make him horny?'

'Yes, I want to see it grow.'

'What shall we do – tickle him?'

'We could try that.'

Silence.

I braced myself, body rigid, waiting for the first contact. 'Girls, please, this isn't funny . . . I don't mind playing games but I want to see what you're *DO* . . . ing!'

Spidery finger tips made the first hit, ran trippingly up my leg and right up The Brute to his chin, then remained there, running on the spot.

Then a hand grabbed him and squeezed him, to the accompaniment of an affectionate murmur.

'Oh, he's lovely,' sighed Clarrie. 'Have a feel, Anthea.'

The hand changed sides, squeezed him, stroked him, then – a gasp.

'Clarrie . . . he's getting hard! I can feel him growing!'

'Let me feel!'

All change again.

'Yes . . . yes! I wonder how much he'll grow?'

A chuckle. 'Hey . . . let's measure him!'

'Yes . . . yes! Go and get the ruler out of his bag!'

Oh, Jeezus . . .

Anthea, I presume, skipped off the bed and fluttered out of the room.

'Clarrie . . .' I panted.

'Yes, Comfort?'

'What are you going to do to me?'

She laughed tauntingly. '*Wouldn't* you like to know.'

'Nothing silly, now . . . I mean, don't . . . hurt him.'

'Oh, as if we'd do that. We love him . . . he's our friend . . . aren't you, little friend?'

She gave him a stroke and tickled his chin again. 'He's growing awfully big . . .'

'Clarrie, take this pillow-case off, *please* . . .'

'No, not yet.'

'Why?'

'Because we want to *tease* you. It won't be half as much fun if you can see what we're doing. We've been planning this a long time, Anthea and I, for the first available man. And you're he, aren't you lucky? We've never had a really good *look* at one, and we want a nice, long play. Would he like a kiss, do you think? Would you, baby? Clarrie's going to give you one, whether you like it or not.'

She moved. I could feel her hot breath on my thigh . . . then her lips touched him. Three . . . four . . . five little pecks, then in he went.

I gasped, raised to meet her.

'Ah, he likes that,' she whispered.

'Hey, what are you doing?'

It was Anthea, back with the ruler.

'Giving him a little kiss,' cooed Clarrie. 'Come and try it, it's lovely.'

Anthea bounced on the bed. 'Here . . . measure him.'

I felt the ruler jammed into his root.

'Wow . . . seven and an . . . eight! . . . no, a quarter!'

'*Su*-per! We'll have to make notes, Clarrie. We'll keep check all the way to Rome. Heh, maybe we should take in the Arab countries. I hear they run to nine inches there.'

'Who needs it? This one's just dandy.'

'Only as a matter of interest, I meant.'

'Here . . . you want to play with him? Give him a kiss, he twitches beautifully.'

Once again I went through the roof, as Anthea's scalding orifice enfolded him. 'Mmm . . . lovely. I could bite his head off.'

'Hey . . .!' I shouted.

'But, of course, I won't. That would be biting off our head to spite our face. Clarrie. Clarrie . . . I want to use him.'

'Be my guest, cousin. But keep him on the boil for me. Don't get greedy once you're on.'

I was sweating, sweltering, panting. Blood was pounding through my head, rocking my body. They were both going to screw me!

The bed danced as Anthea stood up on it. I heard a swish of clothing as her housecoat dropped to the floor. She straddled me, dropped to kneeling position . . . then slowly lowered herself down, caught hold of Brutus and fed him in, gasping as he entered her.

'Oh, Clarrie . . . he's *gorg*eous! He's so big!' A hand slapped my belly. 'Well, done, Comfort.'

I could say nothing, do nothing . . . so decided to lie back and enjoy it.

'Whooo . . . whooo . . . whooo!' she laughed, bouncing up and down. 'Oh, Clarrie, this is a million times better than those old vibrators. I don't care what the girls say, you can't beat the real thing. How're you doing down there, Comfort?'

'I wish you'd take this damn pillow-slip off, I want to see you.'

'Dirty, that, wanting to ogle naked girls. We are both starks, you know.'

'Aw, come on, girls . . .'

'Shall we, Clarrie? He's been frightfully sporty. I think he deserves a little bonus.'

'All right.'

She knelt at my side, raised my head, and pulled the case off. I gasped, blew, puffed, blinked.

'Better?' she grinned.

By golly, they *were* naked . . . stripped to the buff . . . Anthea plump and huge-breasted, Clarrie less well-endowed but nevertheless all there.

'There . . .' declared Clarrie, rising high above me to show herself fully. 'What do you think about that?'

'Miraculous,' I gulped.

With a laugh she slowly fell forward, stopping herself on extended arms, and fed her right breast into my mouth. 'Now we stop acting the fool and get down to some serious screwing . . .OK?'

I nodded OK.

She slid alongside me and untied my left wrist, gave it a little massage, then leaned across me and untied the right one, feeding me her left breast in the process. Then she slipped off the bed, untied my legs and pulled my shoes, socks, trousers and shorts off. Finally she helped me off with my shirt.

'Hi, down there!' laughed Anthea, giving me a wave. 'Welcome to the club.'

Clarrie lay alongside me again, asking to be played with, so I obliged.

'Really kicky,' grinned Anthea. 'This your first time in a threesome?'

'Yes,' I lied.

'Nice, hm?'

'*Su*-per.'

'You want to watch out when Clarrie comes, she goes a bit wild.'

I looked at Clarrie. She was snarling. 'Are you coming?'

She nodded vigorously, tightening her grip on my arm. 'Ohhh . . . ohhh . . .' she whined.

'Here it comes!' proclaimed Anthea, the sight of Clarrie making it obviously excited her. 'Oh, God . . . Clarrie, I'm with you, cuzz . . . ohhh . . . ohhhh . . .!'

'OHHHHHHHHH!' A double yoker.

Clarrie fell across my chest and Anthea fell on her, both of them chuckling and kibitzing, recovering fast.

'Congratulations,' I laughed.

Anthea sat up, threw back her hair and blew out a breath. 'Wow! Kicky . . . kicky . . . *kicky*!'

Clarrie sat up and kissed my right nipple. 'You're terrif, Comfort.' She threw a glance at Anthea. 'Did he come in you?'

'No! He's holding on like a bloody bulldog!'

Clarrie frowned at me. 'Hey, you're double terrif. Get off, Anthea, I want him.'

Anthea dismounted and they changed places, Clarrie nearly fetching me off as she slid home. 'Easy,' I gasped, 'easy . . .'

She froze until I got things under control.

'OK,' I nodded.

She relaxed with a sigh. 'Oh, *crazy* . . .'

'I want what you did to her,' demanded Anthea, sliding up until her right breast was at my mouth, then changed her mind and threw her leg over me, rose up high above me and cried excitedly, 'No . . . I want it here!'

'Ooh, you crafty bitch!' laughed Clarrie. 'I didn't think of that . . . hey! this is like riding pillion with you back here. Giddup there, boy! Wheee!'

And then they were both riding to hounds, racing hell-bent across a hundred-acre field, taking the jumps with a whoop and a holler, Clarrie out in front by a short head, 'Christ, I'm there . . . I'm *there*!'

Anthea was saying nothing but making an awful lot of noise saying it, and when Clarrie went over the top, she was right behind her.

And this time there was no holding back for me, either.

'Jesus, he's hitting me!' cried Clarrie. 'Ooooh . . . oooh . . . ooooh! Sticky *kicky*, daddy . . .'

We all collapsed in a sweaty heap, panting and laughing.

'Comfort, you're simply splendid,' chortled Anthea, now sitting on my chest. 'Clarrie, I've decided, he's coming to Rome with us.'

'Would you like that, Comfort?' asked Clarrie.

'Girls, I'd be delighted to, but unfortunately I couldn't

possibly afford to, and I wouldn't want to lose this job. Tempting offer, though, by jove, though I probably wouldn't live to see *Paris*, never mind Rome.'

'Aw, did we wear poor Comfort out?' pouted Anthea, stroking my face.

'Only temporarily, girls. We fellas don't recover *quite* as quickly as you, you know.'

'How long will it take?' asked Anthea.

'To recover?' I laughed. 'Depends on the stimulation . . . ten, fifteen minutes.'

'Good. I want some sticky, too.'

Oh, blimey . . .

'Tell you what!' announced Clarrie. 'We'll all have a nice friendly shower and *we* will wash Comfort. And if that doesn't do the trick, my name is not Clarrie Fitzhaigh-Donahue.'

Her name *was* undoubtedly Clarrie Fitzhaigh-Donahue. And it certainly did the trick. I came out of that shower feeling a new man, *and* everything in sight. There simply is nothing like a chummy menage-a-trois for getting a fellow going.

'What *do* you girls get up to at school?' I asked, back in bed once more, sandwiched between them, all of us playing with anything that took our fancy.

'School was a big yawn,' complained Anthea, raining kisses on my stomach. 'There was nothing like you there . . . simply nothing.'

'So, what did you do for sex?'

Clarrie answered. 'Mostly each other. All the girls were dyke – I mean, you had to be – or play with yourself, which is so frightfully nothing.'

'No men at all?' I enquired.

They giggled.

'We tried this with the driving instructor,' laughed Clarrie. 'We kidnapped him in the car and took him into the country. But he was a no-no from the word go. So nervous! He came off in his trousers before we'd even got our panties off. Poor lamb, you should have seen his face.'

'You should've seen his trousers,' said Anthea. 'And the way he walked stiff-legged from the car when we got back, all the way across the courtyard. We didn't see him again. We think he resigned that afternoon.'

'You devils,' I grinned, jumping because Anthea was no longer kissing my stomach. 'Hey, down there . . .'

'Ooh, goody, it's sticky time again!' whooped Clarrie.

'My turn this time,' declared Anthea.

'All right, but I want to watch.'

'So, watch.'

'Wish we had a camera, I could take some super snaps. We could take them with us to Rome, then you'd always be in our thoughts.'

'I hope I always will be, anyway.' I said.

'Of course you will, dear Randy,' said Anthea, sprawling on her back. 'Now come and give me a prezzie to take with me . . , and we'll see what we can find for you.'

It was nine o'clock when I finally got out of there, and only then because the minxes were off to a disco to dance the night away (training for their European tour).

At the door they kissed me fondly, thanked me profusely, and promised to return for another couple of days at the end of their tour to tell me how they'd got on – *and* to restoke old passions.

'Take good care of yourself, now,' said Anthea. '*And* him.'

'Stay celibate until we meet again,' cautioned Clarrie. 'We will know if you've been unfaithful.'

I raised two fingers, scout-style. 'Nary a bird shall pass my portals, I promise.'

Anthea said, 'We've been wondering what to give you as a keepsake, something besides memory to remember us by . . . and we've decided on these.'

She brought a little parcel from behind her back and handed it to me. 'Don't open it until you get home.'

'Aw, girls, that's very nice of you . . .'

She pecked me on the cheek. 'It was very nice of *you*.'

'*Su*-per,' said Anthea, taking her turn.

'Have a lovely time, girls, and drop me a line when you're coming back, I'll have a week in bed to build my strength up.'

'Ciaou,' they said. And waved me down the corridor.

I bought some fish and chips on the way home, made a cup of tea and opened the parcel while I was eating.

What a lovely thought, two pairs of frilly panties, one with a cock rooster on the front, the other bearing a fireman's helmet.

And under them . . . a gold Dunhill lighter, inscribed with a letter C. For Clarrie, no doubt, but also for Comfort.

Nice touch, that. I really appreciated it.

CHAPTER TEN

Now I don't want to give the impression that every day at the *Mansions* was a three-ring sex circus, it obviously wasn't. The next day, Thursday, for instance was totally devoid of titillation, and Friday likewise, although Friday brought it's own, different kind of excitement.

Jack Berryweed couldn't wait to give me the good news.

'Morning, Mister Berryweed . . .'

'Here, I've got good news for you, the owners have agreed to let you live in.'

'They have!'

'Yers, phoned through this mornin', said you could have the room in the West Wing. So, you'd better get over there and do some tidying up. Put whatever's in there in the East Wing room. What are you goin' to do about furniture and that?'

I shrugged. 'Buy some . . . on HP.'

'Well, you'd better get along an' do it after you've cleaned out the room. Take the mornin' orf, I'll hold the fort.'

'Thanks very much, Mister Berryweed.'

'Well, it'll make up for all the overtime you've bin doin'. I told the owners all about you, how you've bin workin', and they wus very pleased. So there y'are, you've helped me, now I've helped you. Go on, orf you go. Be back at two.'

With singing heart I raced over to the West Wing, found the room cluttered with boxes of cleaning materials, but had it cleared and swept out in an hour.

It may not have been much by Mansions standards, but it was heaven on earth to me after Mrs Maloney's flea-pit. Nice little room, twelve feet by twelve, with a telephone already installed. And right next door there was a little bathroom, everything just as Jack Berryweed had.

I did a quick calculation as to how much furniture I'd need, then went down the High Street, found a cut-price shop, and ordered a single bed, a nine-by-twelve square of carpet, a chest-of-drawers, a small wardrobe, a bed-side table and lamp, and a little armchair, a hundred and fifty quid the lot.

I was going to put it on HP but when the bloke said he couldn't deliver it for ten days, I ravaged the bank account and paid cash, getting a bit of discount into the bargain, and delivery that same afternoon.

He nearly died when I gave him the address.

After that I strolled back along the High Street, stopping here and there for one or two things, like net curtains and a curtain rail, bedding, a couple of towels, cups and saucers in case I ever had guests, that sort of thing, and arrived back at the Mansions by two.

'Got it all done?' asked Dan.

'All the basics, Dan, and all I can afford right now. The rest'll come later.'

' 'Ere, you want to spread the word around, lad,' he winked. 'Maybe the old girls'll divi up a few bits and pieces.'

'You know, I never thought of that,' I fibbed. 'Good idea.'

'Well, you never know your luck. They may have a Georgian dining suite or a Louis XIVth sofa lyin' around they don't want. Then again they may *not* have, but it does no harm to plant the seed.'

'Indeed it doesn't, thanks for the tip.'

'I, er, expect you'll be doin' some entertaining now, then, will you . . . a little bit of extra-curricula servicing on the side, maybe . . .?'

'Nah,' I grinned. 'I reckon you've got it a bit wrong. I still haven't had the nod from any of them.'

He sniffed. 'Wait till they know you've moved in, mate. They'll be phonin' down for the odd cup of sugar, you'll see.'

'Hope you're right,' I laughed and pushed on.

When I got to Jack's office there was a form to sign, transferring the phone to my name.

'Jot down the calls you make on the company's be'alf,' he said. 'They don't expect you to pay for them, naturally.'

'I'll get a book for them.'

'Right. How d'you get on with the furniture?'

'Fine – they're delivering this afternoon.'

He gave a chuckle. 'Blimey, you didn't waste much time. Reckon you're in a bit of a hurry to move in, eh?'

'I'm in a lot of a hurry to move out of where I am. Will it be all right if I move tomorrow?'

'Any time you like, son, you've got the all clear.'

'Then I'll be over first thing tomorrow.'

The van with the furniture arrived at four, and Jack gave me the last hour off to get settled in. The carpet, naturally, went down first. It was brown with a cream pattern, nice and bright. Then the other stuff went in and by half four I had a palace.

I invited Jack over to have a look at it.

'Well, you've done yourself proud,' he chortled. 'All you need now is your tellie and you're home and dry.'

I couldn't agree less. It was certainly not my intention to sit at home and watch tellie at nights!

'What you going to do about cooking?' he asked.

'I'm not, Mister Berryweed. I'll eat out.'

Or in, I thought, thinking of Mrs Dexter, Billy Chang etcetera, etcetera. Anywhere but in my room.

'What, not even a cuppa tea?' he asked, aghast.

'Oh, yes, that. I've got an electric kettle and things over at my digs. I'll be bringing it all over tomorrow morning.'

'Yes, well . . . looks like you've got yourself a nice little place. I'll have to come over and christen it with a light ale or two.'

'Of course,' I laughed.

Once, I thought. I wasn't having Jack popping in every five minutes.

He toddled off after that and I had a quiet ten minutes to myself, getting used to it. I sat in the armchair and smoked a fag, finding myself very excited with my new place and wondering what scenes of unbridled whooppee the armchair would witness before I was a year older.

What a set-up, I pondered. I was here! – right on the doorstep, ready at a moment's notice to serve any and all, at all times of the day and night. Randolph Comfort Incorporated – at your very service.

I couldn't wait to get started.

It seemed strange, entering that smelly, scrofulous lobby for the last time. Old Faggot Maloney was on the wall phone, screeching abuse at someone who'd had the temerity to call a Miss Sukawara in Room Seven.

'Lissen, I don't care *wot* she told you, she's not bloody in! . . . I *'ave* just knocked on 'er door, man, and she's not *in*! Oh . . . stuff!'

She slammed the receiver into the hook. 'Bloody wogs, can't understand a word of English.'

'Oh? They understand it well enough when you ask them for the rent, Mrs Maloney. Leastwise they always hand it over, don't they?'

'None of your business, Mister Smarty, you just keep your nose *out*.'

'Ah, if only I could, Mrs Maloney. I would like to detach it before entering these portals and leave it on the doorstep overnight, anything to avoid inhaling this hallway.' I gave a sniff. 'What air-freshener have you been using today . . . Essence of Sick or Eau de Jockstrap?'

'Yuh cheeky monkey, I'll . . .'

She went for me with a flat-hander but I ducked and skipped up the stairs. 'I'm moving out tomorrow, Mrs

Maloney, at nine, so the Housing Inspector should be here by ten. And have *you* got a busy night ahead of you!'

I entered hell for the last time, spent two hours packing all my bits and pieces, made myself a cup of char and lay on the bed, saying a soldier's farewell to the cracks in the ceiling.

Goodbye grot; hello Mansions. What a turn-about in one short week.

I reviewed the past seven days, marvelling that so much could have happened since last Friday . . . Mrs Widdlespoon . . . Mrs Dexter . . . Fran . . . Clarrie and Anthea. What a week, and what a haul!

And to think I'd only just begun to tickle the surface.

Once again I took out the list Dan had prepared for me and ran my eye down the list of names and his comments opposite each.

Apartment One, Maxwell B. Frick, American, owns his own advertising agency. Careful when you bend down to pick up your wrench!

Yes, I knew there had to be one around.

Apartment Two, Miss Eleanor Soper. Seventy. Retired . . . rich. Owns two Corgies. Walkies, walkies?

Apartment Three, Mr and Mrs Charles Dexter. Financier. Often abroad. Mrs D makes things to pass the time, like you maybe? Ha ha!

I laughed at that one. I could afford to.

Apartment Four, Count and Countess Rubjortoff. European title, not worth a damn. His title, her money. He 65? She 25? . . . and 36–22–36. Belter. Ex-showgirl. Keep one eye on the Count, terribly jealous.

And so on and so on, all the way through to Apartment Fifty Four, Lady Lovey Glenbullen, gay divorcee. 36? You've seen her so get stuck in. What can you lose but your job? Ha ha.

I lowered the list with a sigh. Possibilities . . . endless. All I had to do was keep my nose clean. What had I made (in cash terms) during the past week? Forty five . . . fifty . . .

sixty . . . eighty, yes, eighty quid, plus two silk shirts, a silk dressing gown, and a gold-plated Dunhill lighter.

Unbelievable.

And now I was actually moving *into* the Mansions.

I got out my Accounts Book and Diary and spent an hour writing up the first week, then, with a grin to myself, put them away, wondering what stories they would have to tell by the end of my first year.

The mind boggled.

CHAPTER ELEVEN

At nine the next morning I was coming down the stairs for the very last time with my cases and carrier bags, sniffing as I reached the hall. By Harry, the old bag had actually sprayed the place with pine freshener. She hadn't *washed* it, mind, just sprayed.

'Ah, you're off, then,' she said behind me, making me jump.

'As much as it breaks my heart, yes, I must tear myself away.'

She eyed the cases suspiciously. 'You taken anything of mine?'

'Hardly. I've even done a stock-check on the cockroaches, they're all up there, just as I found them.'

'You cheeky sod . . .'

'Goodbye, Mrs Maloney . . . give my condolences to your husband.' I was down the steps before she could swipe me with her rent book.

I hailed a taxi and arrived in style, finding a new bloke on the gate, though Dan had primed him that I was moving in and I had no trouble getting through.

Three minutes later I was opening the door of my new home, glad to be there.

There were, incredibly, three notes on my carpet, shoved under the door. I dropped my bags, closed the door and opened them.

The first one read: Ring Apartment Three. The second one read: Welcome to the Mansions! Fran. And the third: Give me a ring. Billy Chang.

I settled in the armchair, lit a ciggie and dialled the internal number for Apartment Three.

Mrs Dexter answered.

'Goodmorning, Mrs Dexter. Randy Comfort here . . .'

'Randy, how are you?'

'I'm just lovely, Mrs Dexter.'

'No doubt of *that*. I saw the furniture van arrive yesterday and presumed you were moving in. How wonderful. Are you speaking from your room now? Where is it?' she sounded excited.

'Not fifty yards from where you're standing, Mrs Dexter, just off the hall in your block.'

'Oh, Randy, how clever of you. I'd love to see it sometime.'

'I'd like that very much, Mrs Dexter.'

'May I have your extension number?'

'199. Please feel free to call any time, Mrs Dexter.'

'How sweet you are. I've found a few nice things for you, Randy. Perhaps you'd like to pop along, say, Tuesday evening and collect them? I'm away all week-end. About eight o'clock Tuesday. How would that suit?'

'Perfectly, Mrs Dexter.'

'See you at eight, Good*bye* . . . Randy.'

I put the telephone down, chuckling to myself. Berr . . . *rum*-te-dum-de-dum. The way things were shaping up, I'd have to get a bigger wardrobe and chest-of-drawers . . . maybe a bigger room!

I dialled Apartment Five and got Billy Chang.

'Mister Nicopopolous's residence.'

'Bet you can't say that when you're pissed,' I said.

'Randy? Hey, you made it! Are you in now?'

'Right down below you, cock, just off the hall.'

'Fantastic. Listen . . . what're you doing tonight?'

'Hang on, I'll consult my appointments book.'

He laughed like he thought I was joking.

'Tonight . . . I'm free.'

'Great. Well, put on your best bib-and-tucker and pop up here at nine precisely – 'cause that's when the dishwasher will be going on the blink. OK?'

'Erm . . .' I was a bit slow. 'How can you know it's going

on the blink at precisely . . . aahh! Silly me! Right, got it. Why, what's happening?'

'A couple of times a year the boss puts on a real knees-up – Christmas time and June, just before we embark for the South of France. And tonight's the night.'

'When are you leaving, Billy?'

'Next week, as soon as he's over his hangover.'

'How long for?'

'The usual three months.'

'You poor bugger.'

'Yeh, rough,' he laughed. 'So, how about tonight?'

'Well . . . terrific, but why me? I mean, hell, he couldn't have invited me . . .'

'No, *I* have. Hence the dishwasher bit. You won't be *in* the party, you'll be in the kitchen with me, but it's something you ought to see. Half the residents in the Mansions will be here and it'll be a good chance for you to have a decko at them, all right?'

'Yeh, great! Thanks a million, Billy. You're sure he won't mind, though . . . ?'

'He'll be so footless he won't even know you're here. This is *the* big one of the year, everybody will be half-seas-over by the time you arrive. It'll be very interesting, take my word.'

'Marvellous. Right, nine it is.'

'Hey . . .' he laughed. 'How did you make out with you-know-who across the way?'

I chuckled filthily. 'I owe you a quid.'

'No kidding! Wey hey . . . ! OK – gotta fly. See you at nine.'

I replaced the phone, realising my face was aching from grinning so much, my mind spinning with excited anticipation. And what would ensue from this little lot? I asked myself.

I busied about getting the room right, unpacked my cases and stowed my clothes away, found a place for my radio and record player, set up the kettle. Then, deciding I needed a couple of shelves, I went along the High Street and bought a couple of plastic-laminated lengths and some brackets, and passed the afternoon installing them.

By seven thirty everything was ship-shape and looked very cozy; nothing fancy, but then again not a place I'd be ashamed to show to any resident who might happen to pop in.

By eight thirty I was showered, shaved and changed, into a dark-brown lightweight suit, cream shirt and patterned, silk tie, and feeling great.

And at nine precisely I was ringing the bell of Apartment Five.

Billy must have been standing at the door, waiting for me. It opened immediately, revealing his welcoming grin and one hell of a lot of party noise in the background.

Jack Berryweed had been right, these flats *were* sound-proofed.

'Good, lad!' he said. 'Quick, into the kitchen!'

We nipped through, heading away from the lounge, the noise decreasing to mere deafening level as we reached the kitchen. The place was unbelievably cluttered, trays of hors d'oeuvres, snacks, sandwiches, and bottles of every drink imaginable filling every square inch of working surface.

'Blimey . . .' I gasped. 'How many people are here?'

He shrugged. 'Sixty . . . seventy. Help yourself to anything you fancy, mate, most of this will be chucked out tomorrow morning.'

'Thanks, don't mind if I do.' I started on the smoked salmon while he poured us a couple of drinks. 'Hey, are you the only one serving, Billy?'

'Not likely. There's two waiters and two waitresses in there, goin' flat out. Right bunch of free-loaders, this lot.'

'Who's here? Just residents?'

He shook his head. 'No, some outsiders, too.' He brought my scotch over, grinning. 'So . . . things went pretty well in Apartment Three, hm?'

'Not bad at all, mate.' I dipped my hand into my inside pocket and extracted a pound note. 'Yours, I believe.'

'Thank you, Randy . . . your agent is mighty appreciative.'

'So is your client. And so is our resident, so everybody's very happy. Keep up the good work. Anything . . . doing to-night, d'you reckon?' I asked, nodding towards the lounge.

'We have a fair sprinkling of possibles. There's Countess Rubjortoff, without the Count. She's a real cracker, lives next door. Ex-showgirl . . . stripper, I believe. Fantastic body.'

'Yes, I've heard about her. I got Dan Brogan to make me a list of the residents with his opinion of each, and he intimated that the Countess was a bit of a belter. But he also said the Count was inclined to be a little jealous.'

'Hey, you've really got things organised, haven't you? A list, yet!'

I sniffed. 'No good doing things by halves, Billy. This is a serious business. Where's the Count, then?'

'In hospital.'

'Eh?'

'Nothing serious, I'm afraid. He pops into the London Clinic for a bit of a rest every now and again. And from the looks of her, I know why! I'd give a month's pay to clobber that.'

'Really?' I mused. 'I must have a decko at the Countess.'

'You will.'

'Who else is here?'

'Tilly Vesper the way-out model from Forty Five. She's a card, that one. Bit of a nutter, but a giggle. Dead Cockney. You'll love her.'

'Sounds good, Billy, go on.'

'Rachel Roget, painter bird from Forty Eight . . .'

'I know her. Not much doing there, mate, I've been. Didn't flutter an eyelash.'

'Don't give up hope. I reckon she's just a bit cautious. She's certainly letting her hair down in there.'

'Yeh? Mmm . . . well, I'll keep an open mind on that. Pray continue . . .'

He couldn't. At that moment the door burst inwards and in waltzed the two waiters carrying empty trays.

'How's it going?' enquired Billy.

'They're shifting a bleedin' mountain of stuff!' panted one, loading his tray with hors d'oeuvres while the other one stacked bottles on his.

Crash!

The door exploded again and in staggered a waitress with a load of dirty glasses and dishes. 'Here, cop this lot,' she said to Billy, and dumped her tray on top of the huge dish-washer.

All three exited, freshly laden.

Billy casually opened the dishwasher, pulled out the racks and began loading the dishes.

'As I was saying before we were rudely interrupted . . .'

We were interrupted again. This time it was another waitress, flushed and breathless, also bearing a heaped tray.

'You Billy Chang?'

'I am.'

'You're wanted in there, lady in a grey silk dress with a split up the side.'

'Oh . . . yes,' he said hesitantly, glancing (fertively?) at me. 'Hang about, I won't be long.'

'Sure.'

Now, what was *this* all about?

When he'd gone, I button-holed the waitress. 'Er, do you happen to know the lady's name, love?'

She shook her head and frowned. 'No, but I think I've seen her before somewhere . . . can't think where, though. Maybe it was another party.' She gave a shrug and left.

Billy was back in a couple of minutes, grinning suspiciously.

'Come on, what's going on?' I asked him.

'Nothing.'

'Cobblers.'

'Nothing, mate, honestly . . .'

I narrow-eyed him. 'Who was the bird in grey with a split up the side?'

'Er . . . Mrs Whatshername from Thirty Eight. It was nothin' – she just wanted to . . .' His face split. 'Look, just forget it . . . wait and see what happens.'

'Billy . . .'

'Forget it! Here, have another drink, we're the only ones sober.'

It was ten minutes before the first one arrived. She was tall, slim as a reed, radiantly red-haired and dressed like Minnie Ha Ha. A real kook.

'Hello,' she beamed, her vivid blue eyes twinkling like a couple of sparklers. 'Anybody got a drink in here . . . Billy, hit me with a scotch, love.'

'Certainly, Miss Vesper . . .'

So this was Tilly Vesper, the model. Ve-ry nice.

She turned the blue, blue eyes on me and smiled alcoholically. 'Hello . . .'

'Hello.'

'You're new. Who are you?'

Billy leaped in, bless him. 'This is Randy Comfort, Miss Vesper. He's our new resident maintenance man.'

She frowned, looked me up and down. 'You don't *look* like a maintenance man . . . you're too beautiful. Maintenance men wear overalls, not suter soups . . . super suits. Oops! I'm pissed.'

'He came to fix the dishwasher but dressed for the occasion,' explained Billy. 'Here you are Miss Vesper.'

She took the drink and sank a sip. 'You fix dishwashers, do you . . . ?'

'He fixes anything,' my agent cut in. 'He's terrific.'

'I have a dishwasher that needs servicing,' she said. 'Billy, give me a fag, darling . . .'

I was there with mine before Billy could move a muscle,

lighting it for her with my gold Dunhill, watching closely as her lush, crimson lips sucked up the smoke.

'I'd be very glad to look at it for you, Miss Vesper,' I said. 'I live on the premises now, extension 199. Please feel free to call any time, day or night . . . I mean evening, of course. If you're working during the day I'd be glad to come up when you get home.'

'I'll think about it. What was your name again?'

'Comfort . . . Randy Comfort.'

'Too much,' she laughed. 'All right . . . I'll call. 'Bye for now!'

With a tiddly wave, she left, the slender mounds of her bottom breathtakingly evident beneath the thin cotton material of her Indian outfit. A fantastic arse.

'Nice, mm?' grinned Billy, reading my mind.

'Wonderful. Tilly Vesper . . . Apartment Forty Five. I shall look forward to servicing her machine with great delight.' I raised an enquiring brow at him. 'What d'you think, agent mine?'

'Weird, is what I think.'

'Really? How so . . . ?'

He laughed. 'Well, doesn't she look it? Last party she came to, she wore see-through pyjamas and bikini knicks – no top. Her nipples were showing plain as day and she didn't give a stuff. She's a terror is Tilly. I reckon you'll be lucky to get out of her place in under a week.'

'Roll on.'

We were discussing the possibility of such a happening when the next one came in.

She was a medium-tall, handsome woman in her late forties, splendidly endowed tit-wise and even more so diamond-wise. She positively twinkled with them. In a knee-length dress of pale green, patterned shantung, her rich brown hair neatly but loosely waved about her benignly smiling face, her bearing was distinguished, confident and immensely self-satisfied. In short, she was loaded.

'Ah, Billy . . .' she declared, her smiling grey eyes addressing me, covering me from top to bottom in one easy scan. 'Hello . . .'

'Good evening, madam.' I inclined my head respectfully.

'Good evening . . . do I know you, young man?'

Again Mister Ten-Percent was there. 'Mrs Harrington-Hartley . . . may I introduce our new maintenance man . . . Mister Randolph Comfort? Randy . . . Mrs Harrington-Hartley . . . Apartment Twenty One.'

'Oh, so *you're* the young man I've been hearing so much about?' she gushed, extending her hand. 'Delighted, I'm sure.'

'I, too, ma'm.'

'Yes, well, no *wonder* the ladies are all talking about you,' she chortled, jingling the jewels on her boobs. 'You're *just* what we've been needing around the Mansions, a touch of glamour. I'm afraid Berryweed *hardly* fills the bill. Well, I'm sure you're going to find yourself *quite* run off your feet, Mister Comfort. I shall have to get my request in quickly before the stampede starts or I shall have to wait months, I have no doubt.'

'Oh, you need something attended to, Mrs Harrington-Hartley? I'd be pleased to put you right at the top of the list.'

'Oh, how *frightfully* kind. I feel honoured indeed. Yes, I do have a little job for you, the carpet in my lounge has come loose and needs tacking down, otherwise there'll be a dreadful accident. *Would* you be an angel and come first thing Monday morning?'

'Of course. How would nine o'clock suit you?'

'Oh!' she laughed. 'My dear, I said "first thing" Monday, not in the middle of the night! No, make it twelve o'clock, would you?'

'Certainly.'

'Well, I must away and flaunt my triumph . . . goodbye for now.'

As she disappeared through the door, Billy broke into a

despicable throaty chuckle. 'Hee hee hee . . . so who's going to make his agent filthy rich, then?'

'God, you've got a foul mind, Chang . . .'

'*Yers*, haven't I. And what did Dan Brogan say about Mrs Harrington-Hartley?'

I closed my eyes, visualising the list. 'Widow of Supermarket tycoon . . . late forties but well-preserved . . . potty about Siamese cats . . . loaded.'

'The mere bones, but accurate. Well, you've just seen her, what do you think?'

'She hit me for six with all that stuff about me being talked about by all the women. That can't be true . . .'

'Can't it? Lissen, these dames play bridge and drink gin in each other's flats every day of the week and they gossip about everything and anything. Believe me, a tall, dark, handsome stranger in the Mansions would make Number One topic for a fortnight. Sure, they've been talking about you . . . you're the most interesting thing that's happened around here since they kicked that pop star out for running a cat-house.' He swigged his scotch and continued. 'Don't underestimate their boredom, Randy, especially the older ones. They've done everything, seen everything and have everything. Now they get their kicks out of the weirdest things . . .'

'Thanks,' I grinned.

'Nar, you know what I mean . . . they suddenly get excited by a new fad and go mad at it for a time, then find something else. They're like schoolkids. You saw my boss, he's on the Yoga kick at the moment, always standing on his bleeding head. Next week he'll have ditched that and taken up archery or something. They're all balmy. But the point is, *you* are obviously this week's fad! At least among the birds. And you've got to make the most of it while it's all cooking. Next week they may fancy old Berryweed, who knows!'

He was telling me nothing I didn't already know, but I continued to play it cool. The boyishly sly, deferential act I was putting on seemed to be working a treat and I wasn't going to change a thing. All I was concerned about was making it last longer than a week . . . a lot longer!

It was when the third one arrived that I began to get the feeling that this passing parade was no accident. Then I began to wonder again about Billy and 'the lady in the grey silk dress with the split up the side', and about his remarks when he'd returned, and I suddenly knew it was for this procession of casual introductions that he'd invited me up.

But had *he* invited me up? Or was he merely fronting for someone else?

Who *was* this bird in the grey silk dress with the split up the side?

This one was a swinger . . . late thirties, plumpish, short, dark hair, looking very chic in a black, embroidered Manderin suit and lots of gold dingle-dangles. She looked a right boozer . . . and a right everything else. *Very* sexy.

'Anybody home?' she called, popping her head in. She spotted me and gave me a cheeky grin. 'Hi, there . . .'

American.

'Hello.'

'Hello, Mrs Gillis,' waved Billy.

'You seen my side-kick around, Billy? I've lost her.'

'Mrs Hungerford? No, Mrs Gillis . . . not for some time.'

'Wonder where that crazy dame's got to? Probably asleep in one of the bedrooms, we had kind of a big night last night.'

'Oh, Mrs Gillis, you haven't met Randy Comfort, have you? He's our new resident maintenance man.'

'Oh, really!' She came right into the room, little plump hand extended, six rings on each finger and another fortune on her left hand. 'Well, hi . . . glad to know you, Randy. They told me a big, gorgeous hunk had taken the job, but I didn't believe it. Now I apologise for my lack of faith.'

'Thank you, Mrs Gillis.'

'You've moved in already, huh?'

'Yes, this morning. I'm right underneath you and Mrs Hungerford, on the ground-floor in this block.'

Her eyes lit up. 'Hey, now how do *you* know where Pam and I live?'

'I've memorised the entire building, Mrs Gillis. It helps me to do the job that little bit better.'

I'd memorised these two all right, mostly because of Dan's remarks.

Apartment Fifteen, Mrs Betty Gillis. American. Divorced. Late thirties. Full-time, good-time flirt and professional party-goer, in partnership with:

Apartment Sixteen, Mrs Pamela Hungerford. Ditto above but blonde. Has a lean and hungry look in the presence of a man, any man! Watch out for these two or you'll be seeing *stars* and putting ointment on your *stripes*! Ha ha.

'Hey, you're *cute*!' she laughed, displaying a faultless set of choppers, her dark eyes flicking all over me. 'I'd better keep you hidden from Hungerford or the Mansions may be missing a maintenance man. Say, now I come to think of it, I've got a little *job* for you . . . freezer door came off in my hand just this afternoon. Could you fix it for me, honey?'

'Of course, Mrs Gillis, any time you like.'

She threw a wink at Billy. 'How about right now!' she said and roared with laughter.

'What's all the hilarity?' drawled a voice from the doorway. 'Am I missing somethin' dirty, Gillis?'

Dan was right, she was lean and hungry-looking. Good face with a strong mouth and jaw. Might be an ex-model. She entered, cutting quite a figure in a gold trouser suit, her bleached blonde hair tied back in a half ponytail, emphasising the cleanness of her jawline.

'What's *this* you've found Gillis?' she grinned, creeping up. 'A *man*?'

'He's a man, honey, and I *did* find him. Just bear that in mind, huh!'

'Hi,' she smiled, flinging a thin, well-tanned arm at me. 'Pam Hungerford, Sixteen.'

'Randy Comfort, your new maintenance man,' I grinned, and was deafened by the screech.

'No! Well, waddya know . . . Gillis, I just found our new maintenance man!'

'Keep back, Hungerford, he's all mine! He's gonna fix my freezer door.'

'Not before he mends my kitchen cupboard! Honey, would yuh?'

'Certainly, Mrs Hungerford.'

'There yuh go, Gillis, he prefers *my* cupboard to *your* freezer door. The guy's got taste, you can see that just by looking at him. Hey, Randy, do you like American pancakes?'

'Love them.'

'Yuh got them. I'll make you all you can eat. Don't eat Gillis's, they'll give you chronic heartburn.'

'*I've* got more than *pancakes* in mind for him,' retorted Gillis. 'Randy, do you like ice-cream? Eighteen kinds I got in my place. Take my advice and leave her pancakes alone, for the good of your health.'

They went on kibbitzing like this for a few more minutes, before Pamela finally hooked her arm in her friend's. 'Come on, Gillis, let's get back to the party and leave the poor guy alone, he'll think we mean it.'

'I sure hope he does,' Gillis said, winking at me. 'I'm serious.'

'See you later, Randy,' laughed Pamela. 'What number do I call?'

'Extension 199, Mrs Hungerford, any time, day or night.'

'Ooh, you *naughty* man.'

'One nine nine,' repeated Betty Gillis, committing it to memory. 'You'll be hearing from me. 'Bye, now.'

They exited, laughing.

'Phew!' I said to Billy. 'What a duo! Imagine both of them getting at you?'

He sighed longingly. 'Yeah . . .'

'Well, well, well . . . things seem to be moving along very

nicely. I reckon that by the time you come back from the South of France, mate, I'll either be three stone heavier or dead from exhaustion.'

All he said in reply was, 'Have another drink,' confirming my suspicions.

It was half an hour before the next one came in but the wait was more than worth it.

Countess Velvet Rubjortoff (neé Velvet Wild – stripper – I was later to discover) was a bomb-blast of a blonde who exploded into the room in a tomato-red cat-suit, stayed less than a minute, but left me limp with desire for the rest of the evening.

She came for ice.

And left with my earnest assurance that I'd be only too *delighted* to fix a new plug on her hair-dryer.

I had to sit down after she left.

'Another drink, Randolph?' grinned Billy.

'Christ, I need one. Aw, mate, this is too good to be *true*! I'm dreaming . . . did you ever see such a bird?'

'I'll be seeing a beach full of them next week. Here, get this down you, you look quite pale.'

I lit a fag with a shaking hand and sat there reviewing the parade, beginning to wonder whether I hadn't bitten off a touch more than I could chew, when suddenly Billy, who had perched on the end of a table, came to his feet and grinned in the direction of the door.

I turned . . . and all the pieces of the jig-saw fell into place. For slinking towards me, looking *outstandingly* sexy in a tight-fitting grey silk gown with a split up the side, was none other than . . . Veronica Dove.

'Out!' she smiled at Billy, jerking a thumb over her shoulder.

As Billy left, I stood up.

'Hello, Handsome,' she husked, 'what are you doing here?'

I met her smile. 'You ought to know, Miss Dove, you invited me.'

She nodded. 'Smart. I knew you weren't just a pretty face. Well, one good turn deserves another – this is your little reward. I told you I'd spread the word around.'

'Thank you very much.'

'Got a cigarette?'

I gave her one, and as I lit it with the Dunhill, she caught my hand and removed the lighter from it. 'Gold, yet . . . and monogrammed. A present?'

'Yes, Miss Dove.'

'Lucky you . . . and lucky lady.' She handed the lighter back to me. 'Well, they do say silence is golden. You're going to do all right for yourself, so long as you remember about the silence. I *can* rely on you, can't I, Randy?'

'Totally, Miss Dove.'

'Good . . . I'd like us to be friends.'

'And so would I.'

She gave a little laugh, touched my cheek and winked. 'Ciao, baby . . .'

And then she left.

Billy returned immediately. 'Boy, what an operator. He's only been here a week and already he's got Veronica Dove working for him. What aftershave do you use, Comfort?'

'It's called "Discretion", Billy.'

'Oh, very good.'

'She arranged it all, hm?'

'Yeah! That maid of hers phoned, told me to invite you up tonight. How did you get that much pull, Randy?'

'Dove wants me to be her leading man in her next film, so I'm playing it for all it's worth.'

He grinned. 'OK, so don't tell me.'

'I can't, Billy.'

'No, I know.'

'Well, mission accomplished, I'd better blow. See you in three months, hm? I'll be thinking of you wallowing in all that misery.'

'Same here. And if there's a bronze statue of you on the

front lawn when I get back, I'll know at least you went out with a smile on your face.'

'*And* taking six of them with me. 'Bye, Billy, and thanks a million. Don't forget to drop me a postcard.'

'Sure, I'll write it before we leave. I won't have the time out there.'

I opened the kitchen door and almost collided with a heavenly-smelling, dark-haired creature in a low-cut gown of brown-and-white swirls.

'Ooh!' she laughed, pursing a pretty mouth. 'Hello . . .'

'Hello,' I said, my evening complete.

It was Lady Lovey Glenbullen.

CHAPTER TWELVE

I lay on my bed, listening to the sounds of the party breaking up – to the alcoholic laughter and chatter of guests returning past my window, to the East Wing, and as an exercise I coupled their names with their apartment numbers. Veronica Dove . . . Forty Three, Tilly Vesper . . . Forty Five, Rachel Roget . . . Forty Eight, Lady Lovey Glenbullen . . . Fifty Four.

For the Centre Block there would be Mrs Harrington-Hartley in Twenty One.

And in my own block, Countess Velvet Rubjortoff . . . Four, Mrs Betty Gillis . . . Fifteen, and Mrs Pamela Hungerford . . . Sixteen.

How well it was all coming together. And there were still a pile of residents I hadn't met!

How many? I wondered.

Feeling wide awake, I decided to make a list of all the apartment numbers and to enter against each one the people I had so far met. When I had finished, it looked like this:

1.
2.
3. Mrs. Dexter
4. Countess Velvet Rubjortoff
5. Mr Nicopoppolous
6.
7. Mrs Widdlespoon
8.
9.
10.
11.
12. Mrs Manley (The bridge player)
13.

14.
15. Mrs Betty Gillis
16. Mrs Pamela Hungerford
17.
18.

So, in the West Wing, out of eighteen residents I had so far only met seven. Still eleven exciting possibilities to go!

In the Centre Block I'd fared even worse, or better. The list read:

19.
20. Mrs Harrington-Hartley
21.
22.
23.
24.
25.
26. Viscount Ballymore (Clarrie and Anthea)
27.
28.
29.
30.
31.
32.
33.
34.
35.
36. Mr Gideon (TV Racing enthusiast)

Pretty bleak list, you'll agree. *Fifteen* possibles here.

The East Wing was considerably richer in immediate promise, with thirteen to come.

37.
38.
39.
40. Miss Suzie Drew (Fran!)
41.
42.

43. Miss Veronica Dove
44.
45. Miss Tilly Vesper – Model
46.
47.
48. Miss Rachel Roget – Artist
49.
50.
51.
52.
53.
54. Lady Lovey Glenbullen

Yes, I had a long way to go yet.

I put the list away in the top drawer of the chest-of-drawers where I kept my Diary, Appointments Book and Account Book, and while I was at it I entered Mrs Dexter in for Tuesday evening and Mrs Harrington-Hartley for Monday noon.

And while I was doing this . . . the phone rang.

The effect was shattering.

With thumping heart, I crossed to it, checking the time. It was ten to one! Obviously a wrong number.

'Hello?'

'Hi . . .' The little American word crept into my ear like warm syrup, tripping my switch with its blatant seductiveness. 'Do you know who this is?'

It was an evens guess and I got lucky.

'Mrs Gillis?'

'You doll, you remembered. Are you in bed yet?'

'No, I was reading.'

'What a criminal waste,' she chuckled huskily, really pouring it on. She sounded smashed and mischievous. 'You did say call any time, Randy . . .'

'Oh, yes, certainly, Mrs Gillis.'

'Are you hungry? Did you eat tonight?'

'I had a few bits and pieces at the party.'

'How do you fancy a nice hot cup of real American coffee?'
'Mrs Gillis, I would love a nice hot cup of real . . .'
'Come on up.'

The door opened as I reached it.
'Come in!' she whispered, glancing furtively up and down the corridor.
She'd changed from the black Manderin outfit into an embroidered black velvet housecoat and satin slippers, and looked very nice.
With a playful giggle she closed the door and put her hand on my arm.
'Hey, this is fun. Did anybody see you come up?'
'Not a soul.'
'Not that I give a damn, it's all innocent fun. I had such a good time at the party, I didn't want it to end just yet, know what I mean?'
'Of course, Mrs Gillis.'
'There is simply *nothing* worse than leaving a ball of a party and coming back to an empty flat, everything hits the dust too damn fast . . . come on through to the kitchen . . . so I thought to myself, to hell with it, he looked like the kinda guy that would appreciate a laugh, I'll give him a call . . . I hope you don't mind, honey.'
'Not at all, Mrs Gillis.'
We entered the kitchen.
'That old hag Hungerford had too much to drink and had to hit the hay, otherwise she'd be here, but I know you're too nice a guy to get the wrong idea about this and I'll know you'll appreciate it for what it is, just a bit of post-party fun . . . siddown and talk to me . . . take your coat off and make yourself comfortable, I'll get the coffee . . .' her eyes twinkled, 'or would you prefer something with a bit more bite to it?'
'What are you having?'

'Coffee, with a drop of somethin' in it. Can't *stand* cawfee by itself.'

'Then I'll have the same, thank you.'

'I knew it, you're fun.'

I slid onto a stool and looked around the kitchen, a showpiece in stainless-steel and ceramics, throbbing with gadgets.

'You have a lovely place, Mrs Gillis.'

'All imported, honey. I just had to have my American kitchen.' She poured coffee from a Cona dispenser and slopped in a heavy shot of what looked like brandy, then brought the cups over, weaving nicely. She was well gone.

'There yuh go. Taste that an' tell me you've tasted better, I dare you.'

She settled onto a stool opposite, her housecoat parting to reveal a deep cleavage between chubby breasts. Under the housecoat I was sure she was naked.

'Cigarette?' I offered.

She took one and had trouble locating the flame of my lighter.

'Good party, then, was it?' I asked.

'Great. Pity you couldn't make it for the dancing though, every guy there was in his dotage . . . great on the chat but not so hot on the clinches.' She rattled a laugh. 'That's the one drawback to money, all the guy's that have it are past everything else. Me, I'd swap a few of their millions for a bit of the old razzamatazz. You'll have to hurry up and make your fortune then come dance with us . . . Pam and me, whaddya say?'

'I'd love to, Mrs Gillis.'

'And who are you kidding,' she grinned. 'If you had money you wouldn't be bothering with a coupla frustrated old bags like Hungerford and me, you'd be knee-deep in beautiful young chicks; snake-hipped swingers with long golden hair.'

Too bloody true, I thought.

'Ah, but a few extra years bring their own compensation, Mrs Gillis. A man can feel very comfortable with a lady who

. . . knows what she wants and goes out to get it. Young birds are too twitchy, too full of themselves for comfort.'

'Oho,' she laughed, '*you* will go far! Keep saying things like that and I *may* lock you in and never let you out! Tell me, how *do* you spend your evenings? Got a girl?'

I shrugged. 'Nope.'

She looked at me sideways. 'Aw, come on . . .'

'No, really. I can't afford one. They cost money, you know. No, I . . . sometimes I go down to the pub for a pint . . . or the pictures . . . I read a lot . . . watch tellie when I can. I don't have one of my own.'

'Broke, huh?'

'Stoney,' I laughed. 'I've just cleared out my bank account buying a bit of furniture for my room.'

'You have a nice room down there?'

'Yes, nice enough, Mrs Gillis. When you're passing – pop in and have a look.'

'I may just do that. How's the coffee?'

'Fantastic. It has a most unique flavour.'

'Yeh, don't it, though,' she laughed, dropping ash on her knee.

'You and Mrs Hungerford are very good friends,' I said.

She nodded. 'The best, she's a doll.'

'Did you know each other in the States?'

'Heck, no, we met right here in the Mansions. We belong to the same club, the gay divorcee outfit. She's been solo for four years, now. Me, I'm coming up for my second.'

'Oh, I'm sorry.'

'No need to be, I'm certainly not. I'm having a heck of a sight better time now than I ever did married, believe me. So is Pam. Hell, we're free women! We can do what we like, when we like . . .' she laughed, 'and *who* we like . . .'

Thud! The barb entered my heart.

'Do you think you'll ever marry again, Mrs Gillis?'

'Not to *that* guy, honey . . . nor the guy before.'

'Oh, you've been married twice?'

'Right. Sixteen the first time, damn silly age. That lasted a whole year. He was forty two . . . owned a string of sports stores across the States. After the honeymoon I didn't see him for two months. Then he came home for a wild weekend and disappeared for another three months. That happened twice more before we called it quits. The second time I was twenty five and he was fifty, a movie producer. That lasted ten years, though it wasn't anywhere near as good as it might sound . . . we slept in separate rooms after the first year, which was when I discovered he was humping every damn ingenue actress on the circuit. I stayed because it suited me to stay, until he asked me for a divorce, which he did two years ago. He paid plenty for the privilege, believe me.'

I believed her.

'And what brought you to England, Mrs Gillis?'

'I fell in love with London first time over here, seven . . . eight years ago. You can get awfully tired of California sun. When the bust-up came, I wanted to get a long way gone, so here I am, free, white and thirty seven – though if you breathe a word of that round the Mansions, I'll poison your ice-cream.'

'Your secret is safe with me,' I laughed. 'Close-Mouth Comfort they call me.'

'You're all right, Randy. Have another coffee, or would you prefer just the brandy?'

'Just the brandy, thank you.'

'Yeh, let's cut out all pretence. What the hell, we're old friends.'

She slid off the stool, collected the brandy and two glasses and came back. 'How come a good-looking fella like you is doing a job like this, anyhow? It can't pay too well.'

'No, it doesn't, Mrs Gillis. Oh, I don't know, I sort of drifted into it. But don't get me wrong, I'm enjoying it enormously.'

'What d'you like about it best?' she smiled, pouring the brandies.

'Sitting here, talking to you.'

'You're a real smooth operator, Comfort,' she laughed. 'Don't think I'm being taken in by all that sweet boyish charm, I'm too long in the tooth to fall for that mullarky. But, hell, I like it. What counts with me is whether the guy's good company – and you *are* good company. You're easy-going, attentive, intelligent . . . and damn nice to look at, so why shouldn't I enjoy having you up here? So long as you keep it nice and light and *fun*, you'll be welcome here any old time.'

'Thank you very much, Mrs Gillis.'

'I know you'll play it right, Randy, and not get too . . . pushy. I won't stand for any of that, you know.'

'No, of course, not.'

'Just so long as we understand one another . . . well, cheers!' She raised her glass. 'Didn't mean to bring the party down, but I just wanted to clear the air between us.'

'Yes, of course, cheers.'

'Come on, what say we have a little dance now . . . get things moving a bit. This place is like a morgue.'

We went through to the lounge and she put on a record, a gentle bossa nova, and came over to me, clicking her fingers, 'Da-di-da da . . . da-da di da-da . . . come to momma, you big lunk.'

She melted against me, all soft and warm and spongy under the velvet gown, very tiddly and not giving a damn. 'Hey, you feel good,' she murmured, hugging me. 'A real hard guy.' She looked up at me, her dark eyes slightly adrift from mine, three inches to the left. 'Hey, you're tall . . .'

'Six two,' I smiled, looking down her cleavage. By gum, she had a right old pair.

'So young . . . so beautiful,' she sighed, smiling wistfully. 'I wish I was ten years younger.'

'You're just perfect as you are.'

'Flatterer,' she laughed, hugging me again. 'Mmmm . . . uh! you do feel good.'

'So do you, Mrs Gillis.'

'Do I?' she said flatly. 'Do I really?'

'Of course you do.'

'I'd like to think so, Randy.'

'You have my unqualified assurance on the matter . . .'

She raised her face again, slipped her arms around my waist and held on tight, glueing herself to me from the waist down, a very disturbing position. '*How* do I feel, Randy?'

I grinned at her. 'Like a woman . . . all soft and . . .' I gnashed my teeth, '. . . uumm!'

'Like that, hm?', she laughed. She raised a coquetish brow. 'Do I . . . disturb you?'

I nodded, licked dry lips. 'I'm disturbed.'

'Is your heart beating fast?'

'Ha! Listen to it.'

She placed her ear to my chest and whooped. 'My God, it's banging like a drum.' She looked up again. 'Well, well, well . . . I do believe the guy's turned on!'

This was all too much for the Brute. He wasn't going to take this kind of teasing lying down. He rose to the challenge, thumped her on the thigh for attention and drew her lips into a slow, smouldering smile. 'Ye Gods, the guy *is* turned on,' she whispered, brushing his burgeoning head with her belly. '*Randy*! . . . and you swore you wouldn't get pushy.'

The record came to an end and with a taunting laugh she broke away, giving me a chance to adjust my mate, who was straining to burst my shorts.

She put on another record and turned to look at me, a sexy smile curling her mouth as her eyes fell on him. 'Disgusting. I think we'd better sit down and have a drink, give you time to cool off.'

She didn't mean a word of it.

'Sit there,' she directed, pointing at a long, floral couch. 'I'll get the brandy. And light me a cigarette, hm?'

She disappeared to the kitchen and returned with the bottle, and a folder of some kind. Setting the bottle and glasses on a low table in front of us, she flopped down on the couch, curled her legs under her, drained her glass and poured another, at one point missing the glass completely and flooding the table.

I glanced surreptitiously at her and found her quite cock-eyed, swaying noticeably, unable to focus.

'Shall I get a cloth?' I said.

'Nah, forget it . . .' She turned her attention to the folder on her knee. 'You wanna see somethin' . . . you wanna see a really great-lookin' chick?' She opened the folder and brought out a dozen eight-by-ten stills. 'My second husband was kinda nuts about photographing me . . .an' give him one thing, he was a damn good photographer. What d'you think about that one?'

She passed me the first still. It was herself all right, shot about seven or eight years earlier, I would guess. She was right about the quality of the photography, it was a study in superb lighting technique, and in artistic nudity. She was posed in kneeling profile against an abstract background, the light striking her from height, like a shaft of sunlight through a church window, touching only certain parts of her body, and leaving the rest in darkness.

But in darkness or not, one thing was obvious, she had the most stupendous pair of full-sized knockers and the most perfect body it has ever been my pleasure to fancy. Conservatively I reckoned she'd put on a good thirty pounds in weight since these stills had been shot.

'Somethin', huh?' she smiled.

'Beautiful, Mrs Gillis . . . beautiful.'

'How about this one?'

One by one she passed them to me, each a little more bold than the last, more and more of her being revealed as the lighting and her position changed, until, at last, she was posed in full-frontal nudity, the sight of her profuse, dark, pubic cluster and the distinct cleft of her vulval lips cloying my mouth and getting old Brutus on his hind legs again.

'Ain't she somethin'?' she laughed, her voice cracking, hoarse with drink.

I gulped. 'Exquisite, Mrs Gillis.'

'Does she *move* you, Randy?'

I nodded, sweating now.

She reached out her hand as though to remove the stills from my lap, but went in low and sneaky, making me jump, her hand full on him.

'Jesus, she did move you . . .' She tossed the stills onto the table and returned her hand immediately, caressed him gently and gave him an affectionate squeeze, grinning lop-sidedly at me, or at someone over my right shoulder.

Her voice became a slurred, low-pitched whisper. 'Did you like the photographs, Randy?'

My heart thudded out the words. 'Very much, Mrs Gillis . . .'

'She really turned you on?'

'Yes . . .'

'And the real thing turns you on, hm?'

I cleared my throat. 'Very much . . .'

'Would you like to take me to bed, Randy?'

'Yes . . .' I croaked.

'And make love to me?'

I nodded, unable to speak.

'*How* would you make love to me, Randy?'

'Any . . . any way you wish, Mrs Gillis.'

'Are you a gentle, thoughtful lover?'

'*I* think so . . .'

'Or a wild young bull?'

'That, too.'

'What would you like to do to me, Randy? Tell me . . . whisper in my ear.'

She leaned closer, her hand still stroking, squeezing, her gown opening wide to expose her breasts.

'Well, I . . .' I paused, undid the top two buttons of her

gown and slid my hand inside to take her big, warm, squashy breast.

She looked at me, so closely, her lips parting in a whispered gasp. 'Tell me, Randy . . . tell me!'

I put my lips to her ear and whispered the sweet obscenities she wanted to hear, her hand tightening on me as the promises went deep, seizing her passion and drew it thudding to the surface.

She shut her eyes and uttered a groan. 'Yes, yes . . . do it to me . . . do it to me.'

'Where? . . . here?'

She shook her head. 'No . . .' She released me and tried to get up, fell against me, and tried again, this time managing to get to her feet, though swaying so much I thought she was going to take a header into the carpet.

'Whooo!' she laughed, holding her forehead. 'Randy, I'm biffed! Hold me, hm?'

Tucked under my arm, we made our way into the bedroom, she lying hard against me. 'Oh, *boy*, oh boy . . . am I blitzed!'

'You sure you're all right, Mrs Gillis?'

'Dear Randy, I'm just *beautiful* . . . just get me on that bed and I'll show you how beautiful I am . . .'

We entered the room, the light from the hall sufficient to see by. I guided her to the huge bed and helped her onto it. She hit it like a felled redwood, arms and legs spread wide. 'Oh, beautiful . . . are you there, sweet man?'

'Yes,' I chuckled, stirred by her position of utter abandonment.

'Come here . . .' she patted the bed at her side.

I lay alongside her. 'I'm here.'

She felt for me, her eyes closed. 'You've still got your clothes on. Take them off.'

I nipped off the bed, shed hurriedly, and nipped on again. 'I'm back.'

She felt for me again, ran her hand from my shoulder to

my thigh, nodding approvingly. 'Tha's better. Now . . . undress me.'

There was little to do . . . just six buttons on her housecoat. With thundering pulse and constricted throat I lifted the sides of the garment and threw them aside, my blood going wild at the sight of her nakedness. She was mine . . . all mine, beautifully tiddly, excitingly uninhibited, gloriously wanton.

I lowered my head and took her breast with my mouth, my hand smoothing a path along her voluptuous flesh to the warm, moist paradise between her thighs.

But at the perimeter of her pubic mound I stopped . . . as her first snore disembowelled my passion.

She was fast a-bleeding-sleep!

'Mrs Gillis!' I whispered, aghast. 'Mrs Gillis!'

I gave her a nudge, a shake, a poke, but it was useless. She was dead, and wouldn't resurrect this side of noon, I knew.

I knelt beside her and looked down at her, stirred by her defenceless nudity, yet feeling a heart-tug of pity for her, then, with a laugh and a shake of my head, I closed the gown over her body and refastened the buttons.

While I dressed she didn't move a muscle. I went back into the lounge and hunted for a pen and paper, found them in a bureau, and wrote:

> 'Good morning, Mrs Gillis! Thank you for a lovely evening. I enjoyed myself so much I forgot to fix your freezer door. Perhaps you'd like to give me a call? I'd be glad to do it any time. And how about the ice-cream!'
>
> Randy.
>
> P.S. About the photographs . . . they're not a patch on the real thing. Honest!

I went back into the bedroom, moved a small vase of

flowers from a dresser to her bed-side table and propped the note against it.

'Goodnight, Mrs Gillis,' I said, getting a soft fluttery snore in reply.

Then I returned to the kitchen, collected my coat, and let myself out of the flat . . . feeling so damned pure in heart I couldn't stand myself, but knowing it had all been *very* worthwhile.

CHAPTER THIRTEEN

I slept late, got up at two, went up town to get the Sundays and a bite to eat, and was back in the room at four, reading the News of the World about some dirty unprincipled bugger who'd made love to a forty-year-old widow woman then pinched her life's savings, when there was a knock on the door.

I opened it and got a shock. It was Mrs Gillis, looking very nice in a yellow dress, and a comical grimace, fanning herself meaningfully with my note.

'Hello,' I grinned.

'Hello, yourself.'

'Won't you come in?'

'That's why I'm here.'

She entered, looked around and nodded. 'Hm . . . not bad.'

'Here, sit in the armchair. Would you like a cup of coffee?'

'No, no, I can only stay a minute, I'm going out.'

She flopped in the armchair and looked at me, smiling a tight little smile. 'I, er, got your note . . .'

'So I see.'

'I treated you very badly.'

'You did not. It was late, you were tired.'

'I was not tired, I was stewed. Some hostess . . .'

'You were,' I said. 'I had a great time.'

'If you expect me to deny all knowledge of what happened between us, you're quite wrong . . .'

'I don't. I hope you remember everything.'

'I do.' She laughed. 'Well, most of it . . . it got a bit hazy towards the end. Though I do recall you . . . well, never mind, I haven't come to talk about that. I've come to thank you . . .' she indicated the note, '. . . for this. And for behaving so very gentlemanly.'

'Sshh . . .' I said. 'You'll ruin my reputation round here.'

'*And* to ask you . . .'

'Yes, Mrs Gillis?'

'If you like Southern Fried Chicken.'

'I jurst *lurv* South'n Fraad Chicken. It happens to be mah *favourite* dish.'

'Good. Then you'll come for dinner?'

'Er, certainly . . . when?'

'Tonight, of course. How much longer do you expect me to wait before I get my freezer door fixed?'

'I'm sorry about that. Right . . . tonight it is.'

'Come at eight, not a moment later.'

'Yes, ma'am.'

'I hate Sundays. Don't you hate Sundays?'

'Loath them.'

'In that case, come at seven.'

'Yes, ma'm.'

'Do you play Scrabble?'

'School champion three years running.'

'We'll play Scrabble.'

She stood up and gazed once more around the room. 'It's pretty bleak, isn't it? You could do with some nice pictures . . . and you have no television!'

'No.'

'How can you live here without television?'

I grinned. 'I rely on my memories.'

'Mmm . . .' she moved to the door. 'Then we'll have to provide you with some of those, too, won't we? In that case, see you at six thirty.'

Well, that was two hours ago and the big hand is now creeping up to half past six, so I'm off.

I've spent the past two hours writing up my diary and *pre*-tty interesting reading it makes. But what, I've been asking myself, will it read like by the end of the year . . . and by the end of next year!

If you're interested, I'll let you take a look some time – so watch out for 'The Further Doings of Randy Comfort' – coming soon. And after last night, the sooner the better.

Oh, blimey, there's the phone . . .

'Hello? . . . hel*lo*, Mrs Harrington-Hartley, how are you today? . . . Change it from noon tomorrow to Thursday evening . . . well, now, I'll just get my appointment book and check that . . . Yes, Thursday evening will be perfect, Mrs Harrington-Hartley . . . eightish? . . . certainly. Pardon? Yes, I *adore* steak and chips, it happens to be my *favourite* dish . . .'

Hee hee hee! The rise of Randy Comfort has begun!

I'll let you know how it continues.

Be seeing you!

Memo for Monday: Buy tin of Whiskers for the Harrington-Hartley cats and consult bank manager re investment advice . . . and a sunny tax haven.

THE SWEENEY

Ian Kennedy Martin

Jack Regan is one of the Heavy Mob.
He's also a loner, intolerant of red tape and insubordinate to his superiors.
And he just happens to be the best detective in Scotland Yard's crack Flying Squad.

When Regan receives orders to co-operate with Lieutenant Ewing, over from America to trace a cop killer, Regan is pursuing his own case and ignores them. But he soon discovers that Ewing is as tough as he is – and a dangerous clash of personalities develops. As the two cases begin to merge into a sinister and violent network of IRA provos and murderers, the two men close in for the kill . . .

Ian Kennedy Martin is the creator of Thames Television's enormously popular TV series, starring John Thaw.

FALLS THE SHADOW

Regina Ross

Beautiful Nicola Beaufort is spirited, stubborn, and determined. Top British Intelligence agent Charles Forsyth is tough, resourceful, sardonic and experienced. Their initial encounter at Heathrow Airport is violent and explosive, setting a pattern that is to be repeated in the days ahead in distant Rumania, where both are seeking, for different reasons, Tony Rothman, fellow operative of Forsyth, and former lover of Nicola.

Plunged into a whirlpool of intrigue and violence, Nicola and Forsyth are drawn together against their will in a desperate race to reach the missing agent, as they realize that the key to their search lies in the discovery of the 1,000-year-old Crown of St Stephen, symbol of the Hungarian monarchy, buried somewhere in the heart of the mountains.

VOTE FOR A SILK GOWN

Jay Allerton

Three men wanted her: Max, ironic, witty, tied to a woman he despised, Guy who had loved her from the first moment he saw her, John with the quiet smile . . .

Janet Semple was blonde, intelligent, beautiful and she wanted perfection. When John Robson, the managing director promoted her to be his secretary, she was overjoyed. But the new job became a nightmare, for John Robson, a married man with three children, fell deeply in love with her, and Janet found herself see-sawing between happiness and despair as she realised that she would never be able to face life without him . . .

Winner of the Romantic Novelists Association Major Award for 1974

FLAME AND THE FLOWER

Kathleen Woodiwiss

The Tempestuous epic of America's deep south at the end of the eighteenth century.

Heather Simmons escaped from the drudgery of her aunt's farm to what she imagined would be the magnificence of London high society. Instead she fell into a far more degrading captivity which took her from a squalid London dockside to the splendour of a Carolina plantation, as the unwilling companion of arrogant and devil-may-care Captain Brandon Birmingham. A man who had abducted her, robbed her of her virtue, and sworn never to let her go.

THE WOLF AND THE DOVE

Kathleen Woodiwiss

A novel of stirring passion and adventure set in Anglo-Saxon England.

The Normans swept across England, ravaging, pillaging, murdering, and at last they came to Darkenwald. When the massacre was over, only lovely Lady Aislinn survived to protect her vanquished people from the conqueror, but the price was servitude to Ragnor, one of the most hated knights in William's army

Then Wulfgar, the Iron Wolf of Normandy, came to claim Darkenwald as his prize of war, and Aislinn faced a more terrible bondage still, as she grew to love the enemy warrior who had destroyed her family, degraded her people, and despised her as a slave.

THE FLAME OF THE BORGIAS

Jean Briggs

The torchlight flickered and shone over the figures moving to the swaying rhythms of the dance. Two people met and held each other's burning gaze across the crowded room.

She was Lucrezia Borgia, Duchess of Ferrara, wife to Duke Alfonso, part of a world of intrigue, corruption and violence. He was Pietro Bembo, a nobleman of Venice. Between them blazed a love that if discovered, would spell death for them both. A love that burned from the crenellated walls of the palaces of Ferrara, to the bustling canals of Venice: from glittering formal evenings spent dancing under the malevolent eye of Cardinal Ippolito to nights in each other's arms. A love doomed to destruction.